LEANNE LIEBERMAN

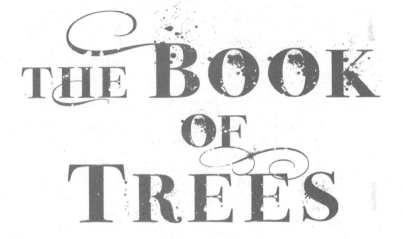

THE BOOK OF TREES

ORCA BOOK PUBLISHERS

Library and Archives Canada Cataloguing in Publication

Lieberman, Leanne, 1974-
The book of trees / written by Leanne Lieberman.

Issued also in an electronic format.
ISBN 978-1-55469-265-1

I. Title.
PS8623.I36B66 2010   JC813'.6   C2010-903598-4

First published in the United States, 2010
Library of Congress Control Number: 2010929059

Summary: When Mia goes to Israel, she gets a crash course in the history
of the Jews in Palestine and starts to question her Zionist aspirations.

Mixed Sources

Cert no. SW-COC-001271
© 1996 FSC

*Orca Book Publishers is dedicated to preserving the environment and has printed this book
on paper certified by the Forest Stewardship Council.*

Orca Book Publishers gratefully acknowledges the support for its publishing
programs provided by the following agencies: the Government of Canada through
the Canada Book Fund and the Canada Council for the Arts, and the Province of British
Columbia through the BC Arts Council and the Book Publishing Tax Credit.

Canada Council
for the Arts

Conseil des Arts
du Canada

ONTARIO ARTS COUNCIL
CONSEIL DES ARTS DE L'ONTARIO

Design by Teresa Bubela
Cover artwork by Janice Kun
Typesetting by Nadja Penaluna
Author photo by Bernard Clark

ORCA BOOK PUBLISHERS
PO Box 5626, Stn. B
Victoria, BC Canada
V8R 6S4

ORCA BOOK PUBLISHERS
PO Box 468
CUSTER, WA USA
98240-0468

www.orcabook.com
Printed and bound in Canada.

13 12 11 10 • 4 3 2 1

For Rob

That which is hateful to you, do not do to your neighbor.
This is the whole Torah; the rest is commentary,
go and learn it. —Hillel

ONE

My first morning in Israel, the guttural wail of the Muslim call to prayer jolted me awake. I sat up in bed and tried to swipe the furry feeling off my teeth with my tongue. My fingers fumbled for my water bottle. Again the call came, so plaintive it made me think of hunger and lost dogs.

My roommate, Aviva, rolled over, mumbled "barbarians" and pulled her sheet over her face. Light bulldozed through the window. I wanted to turn over and sleep some more, but I also needed to explore that sound. I rubbed the heel of my hand across my face. Jet lag made the nerves behind my eyes feel like taut elastic bands.

Aviva and I had arrived in the dark the night before, and I'd dozed in the car from the airport. I remembered seeing the highway lights, and when the road climbed to Jerusalem, I thought of the word *l'aalot*: to go up, as in, up to God.

Our dorm room had two metal beds separated by a desk, two wooden chairs, a closet and a sink. The bathroom and a small kitchen were down the hall. Aviva must have unpacked last night; her makeup and three bottles of hair product took up half the shelf below the sink.

I stepped over my unpacked duffel bag and padded out of our room through a lounge area to a balcony. The B'nos Sarah Yeshiva for Girls, where Aviva and I had come to study, was on the way up to French Hill. Below me the streets descended a terraced slope, each terrace supporting a four- or five-story stone building. At the bottom of the hill, sand stretched into a deep valley dotted with villages. A minaret blared the call to prayer. Beyond the villages, the yellow hills of the Judean Desert rolled into the distance.

I held my breath. This wasn't the land of milk and honey, but the land of sand, sand, sand. "Holy shit," I whispered. There was probably a blessing for such a beautiful sight, but I didn't know it, so I sang a little bit of "Amazing Grace."

Back in our room, I put on my running clothes, ate a stale roll from my backpack and left a note for Aviva. Outside, a breeze chased away the night's cool dew, bringing with it the heat of the desert. The sun bore down, dazzlingly bright, reflecting off the walls of Jerusalem stone. I jogged by more four-story apartment buildings, a grocery store and a bank until I came to a little park with bushes and benches. I stopped to stretch my calves. Again, the desert landscape spread before me. I wanted to run into the sand, to stand in all that space, that emptiness.

I chanted the first morning prayer, "*Mo dei ani lefanecha*." Thank you for returning my soul to me. I recited other prayers from memory, adding little bits in English. "Thank you for waking me up to see the desert in the morning."

When I got back to the dorm, sweaty and elated, Aviva was applying anti-frizz to her brown curly hair, peering into a tiny lighted mirror set in a pink plastic makeup box. She looked up. "I was starting to worry about you. You were jogging?" She looked incredulous.

Aviva was petite, with a small elfin face, a pointed chin and crooked eyeteeth. Her nails were always manicured, her blouses and long modest skirts ironed and spot-free. Aviva was super-smart and knew tons about Judaism, yet she was totally sheltered. She'd lived all her life in Toronto and never taken the bus or subway alone. Regular things like movies, soap operas or MTV were exotic to her. We'd met six months earlier at her parents' house when I started learning about being Jewish. When Aviva suggested I come to the yeshiva with her, I didn't even know what that meant. But now, here I was, just graduated from high school and spending two months at a seminary in Jerusalem before I started university. Even I couldn't believe it.

I took a drink from my water bottle. "I didn't want to wake you, and I had to go out and explore."

"How did you know where to go?" Aviva carefully slid a rainbow-colored plastic headband into her hair.

"Oh, I just went down the road one way and then retraced my steps." I lay down on the floor to stretch my hamstrings.

"You should be careful where you go."

Even though Rabin, Arafat and Clinton had all witnessed the signing the Oslo Accords a few years earlier, all through 1995 there'd been a string of bus bombings in Israel. I got up off the floor with a little leap. "I'm sure I'll be fine."

Aviva frowned, but I could tell she was also impressed. "So how was it?"

"Hot. Amazing." I grinned wildly. "I never knew the desert could be so beautiful."

Aviva clasped her hands together. "I knew you'd love it here. Do you want to go to the *Kotel* today?"

"Sure. What's that?"

"Oh." Aviva looked surprised. "It's, you know, only the holiest place in Israel, the last wall of the temple."

"Oh, you mean the Western Wall. Yeah, sure. The *Kotel*. Is that how you say it in Hebrew?"

Aviva nodded.

By the time I showered, dressed and ate breakfast, the temperature had soared. The scorching air felt like a smoky cloud. On the bus I gawked at the stone buildings, the traffic, the different kinds of people: religious men wearing *kippahs*—small cloth skullcaps—teenage soldiers with huge guns, and ordinary loud kids with big backpacks.

The bus dropped us off at the Jaffa Gate of the Old City. On one corner, buses and cars spewed exhaust. Across the street, a massive stone wall encircled the ancient city of Jerusalem. Shivers ran down my sweaty spine. So much for showering.

I followed Aviva through the shady gate and into the Old City. Inside, the sun bounced off the plate glass windows of money changers, jewelry shops and tour agencies. I pivoted, turning in a circle, feeling the slipperiness of the stone road. A man sold bread sticks from a cart in front of a huge stone citadel. I watched a tour guide herd a throng of middle-aged tourists in wraparound sunglasses and safari hats down a narrow alley.

"Come," Aviva said. "This is nothing."

She led me through an archway and into a tunnel that opened onto a road so narrow I had to sandwich myself against the stones when a car drove by. "We're heading into the Armenian section now," Aviva explained. "It's the fastest way to the *Kotel*. The other way, you go through the Arab *shuk*—the market. It can be dangerous."

I had trouble keeping up with Aviva. I wanted to go slowly and take it all in. Tourist shops sold blue and white Armenian pottery, cheap pens, postcards and *I Heart Israel* hats. A blister flared on my heel from my new sandals, and my underwear became a sweat-soaked wedge between my bum cheeks. The heat, or maybe the jet lag, made me dizzy.

Then Aviva turned down a lane lined with tiny grocery stores. I stopped to peer into a newspaper cone of spice. "Zatar," Aviva said. "You can try it another time." The road opened up to a square full of jewelry stores and pizza places. In the distance I saw a stone arch, a semi-circle of Jerusalem stone.

"That's the Hurva Synagogue." Aviva pointed. "The *Kotel* is just around the corner." We went down another narrow path, and then suddenly we came to a large balcony crowded with people.

"Now"—Aviva beamed—"go as slow as you like."

The crowd shuffled toward a balcony railing. Aviva pointed. "That's the *Kotel*. Isn't it amazing?"

I nodded, but I wasn't looking at the giant stone wall with weeds growing in the cracks. Above the wall a beautiful golden dome glinted in the sunshine. I drew in my breath and pressed myself against the railing. "What's that?"

"Oh, that's the Dome of the Rock."

I'd read about the Dome in my guidebook. Muslims believed Mohammed had gone up to heaven from a rock inside the shrine. The golden globe rested on its blue mosaic base like the sun setting over a lake. Oh my god, what a gorgeous building. I felt like I was splitting in two, like seismic plates were passing by each other and an earthquake was happening inside me. I thought, I'm gonna divide my life into before and after this moment. I didn't know anything about Islam, but I thought Muslims must love their religion not only because of heavenly promises—wasn't there something about virgins in heaven?—but because of this shimmery jewel of gold and aquamarine, this oasis for the senses in a city of white buildings and yellow and brown dirt.

I could have stayed on the balcony forever, but the crowd moved forward, down a set of stairs onto an enormous plaza in front of the wall. Yeshiva boys in their uniform white shirts and dark pants mingled with dorky-looking tour groups in matching sunhats and old lumpy women swathed in scarves. Ultra-Orthodox Jews, or *chassids*, congregated in their eighteenth-century knickerbockers, ringlet sidelocks dangling under their fur hats. As we made our way across the plaza, I noticed a fence dividing the wall into a large men's section and a much smaller women's section. Aviva joined the sea of backs bobbing and swaying on the women's side. I sat in a chair in front of the wall on the women's side to take it all in.

Women pressed against the massive stone in a tight row. Up above, soldiers stood on top of the wall. I wanted to stand up there with them and look down on both the Jewish and Muslim sides. A hovering Christian tour group distracted me. What did they think of all this? I was dying to stop a women in an orange T-shirt proclaiming herself *A Proud Member of the Mississippi Baptist Congregation* and ask her…ask her what? I tried to stop thinking. I mean, I was at the *Kotel*. I wanted the moment to fill me with holiness. I took a few deep breaths and tried to feel the history of the place. Generations of Jews had prayed here, brought sacrifices here. The high priest came here to talk to *God*. I took a deep breath, but I still felt like my same old self.

A spot along the wall became empty, so I crammed myself between two sweaty bodies and joined the line of women jammed against the stones. Up close, the wall seemed like any other Jerusalem stone wall except for the notes wedged in the cracks. Around me women prayed like pilgrims after a long journey. I rested my hands on the warm stone. "This is home," I whispered. But it wasn't. It was just a stone wall in a very hot foreign country.

I felt so empty my eyes started to well up. I swallowed back tears. Damn, I was not going to cry. I took out my prayer book and mumbled my way through the afternoon prayers as best I could, switching between the still-unfamiliar Hebrew and the repetitive English, trying to block out the murmurings of the women around me. When I was done I backed away like the other women were doing, which I thought was kind of stupid because I didn't think a *wall* really cared if you turned your back. Of course I knocked over a chair on my way out, which is what happens when you try to walk backward in a crowded place.

Aviva was waiting for me across the plaza on a bench in the shade. "So, how was it?" She leaned forward eagerly.

"Good, great."

"Is it like you thought it would be?"

"I don't know." I put on my best fake smile. "There are a lot of people here."

Aviva squished her sunhat in her lap and tapped her sandals on the stones. "I like to think about the soldiers who first got here after the '67 war. How exhilarating that must have been. To want something and fight for it, and then finally have it."

"Yes, if you fought for something…"

"We're so lucky now. Everything is given to us. Other people fought for Israel, and all we need to do is come." Aviva hugged herself.

I nodded.

We sucked on our water bottles and watched the tourists. I listened to a guide explain the excavation of the Cardo, a Roman ruin, to a group of elderly tourists. Sandals slapped across the stones.

Maybe I didn't want Israel badly enough. Maybe if I had struggled to get here, it would mean more.

Aviva stood up. "You look tired."

"I'm so exhausted I could cry."

"It's the middle of the night for us."

"Don't tell me."

"Let's go. We can explore another time."

On the way back through the Armenian quarter, I saw a beautiful church. "Hey, can we stop a moment?"

Aviva crinkled her brow. "In a church?"

"It looks beautiful, and it's probably cool."

"Neh. I wouldn't be…comfortable."

"Oh." I thought about asking why, but I was too tired.

✦

We slept through the rest of the hot afternoon with the whirr of the fan over our heads. I dreamed of heat I could see in waves. I woke to Aviva insistently shaking my shoulder. "It's time to get up for Shabbos," she said.

"Forget it." I rolled over in my sweaty sheets, brushing hair off my face. "I'll celebrate another day."

Aviva flicked on the lights. "We need to get ready."

Shabbos, the day of rest, began on Friday night. Once the sun went down, no work, including cooking, cleaning, driving and even turning lights on and off, could be done until sundown the next night. The rules and rituals were still new to me.

Aviva poked my foot. "C'mon, there'll be dinner and you'll get to meet a bunch of new people."

I tugged the sheet over my head. "I already know people." Jet lag made my body ache.

"Here." Aviva thrust a glass of water at me. "Drink this and you'll feel better." I sat up in bed and drank, and I did feel better.

I showered and changed into a pale blue blouse with a sequined butterfly over one breast and a light pink skirt with a layer of tulle underneath. I wore cute little ballet flats and piled my hair on top of my head to get it off my neck. Aviva waited patiently as I applied eye shadow the same color as the skirt. I held up a little jar of makeup sparkles. "Want some?"

"Um, no, that's okay."

I brushed a few over my cheeks and followed Aviva down the stairs of our dorm, through the courtyard and into the main B'nos Sarah building. We walked through the lobby and up a flight of stairs to a large room lined with books. Groups of girls talked excitedly between rows of chairs. Aviva tapped one girl on the shoulder and the girl turned around and screamed, "Aviva!" They hugged and kissed.

The room grew noisier and hotter as more girls and women entered. Fans spun uselessly in the thick air. I started to sweat, but I didn't care. The girls' excitement was infectious, and even though I didn't know anyone, I felt happiness saturate me. The light streaming through the windows from the setting sun looked different, as if it was a holier color than the sun at home.

A line of girls came in through the double doors, dancing and singing a Hebrew song, the last girl playing a violin. Everyone formed a circle and started doing a grapevine step, twisting and turning and singing, "*Hava nagila.*" Someone grabbed my hand and pulled me into the circle. The song repeated and I joined in, letting my voice sound out loud and clear, even though I didn't know what the words meant. Girls broke off from the main circle and made smaller inner circles.

When the dancing stopped, everyone filed into the seats and evening prayers began. All around me, female voices rose: devoted, intense, happy. I sighed deeply despite my exhaustion. I was in Israel, I was Jewish and I was surrounded by Jews who all loved Israel, who all loved *Hashem*—God. A few tears crept out of my eyes, and this time I let them streak down my face.

Aviva smiled at me and gripped my hand. "I knew you'd love it here."

I gave her a huge hug. "I didn't know Israel would be so amazing."

TWO

Classes began on Sunday, the first day of the week in Israel. Aviva led me through the crowded lobby of B'nos Sarah to sign up for my schedule. I nervously adjusted the belt of my red-and-white-checkered dress. All the other girls wore long straight skirts and loose pastel tops. Shit. Tomorrow I'd wear my cream skirt with the pockets.

Aviva guided me to an office and introduced me to a middle-aged woman named Rochel. I tried not to stare at her fake-looking blond wig. Married Jewish women covered their hair for reasons of modesty. Most women wore a hat or a scarf, but really religious women cut their hair and wore wigs. It totally weirded me out.

"Welcome to B'nos Sarah." Rochel smiled. "Are you interested in a full-day schedule or half?"

Aviva headed off to her own lesson, and Rochel handed me a brochure filled with pictures of happy girls bent over textbooks. I looked over the beginner program.

"I'm here on scholarship," I told Rochel.

"Wonderful. You can take as many classes as you like. The evening lectures and workshops are free too."

"I'm only here for the summer…"

Rochel looked me straight in the eye. "Then you should definitely study as much as possible. Your return is equal to your investment."

"Oh, I see. Can I sit in on a few classes?"

"Of course." Rochel took out a pen and started writing room numbers on a sticky note. "You've missed biblical Hebrew, but you could slip into the beginner prayer class and then the Torah lesson. Then there's a half-hour break, and at eleven thirty you can go to *halacha*, the law class. Come talk to me after that if you want to stay for the afternoon." She handed me the sticky note and beamed.

I made my way upstairs to the correct classroom and quietly slid in the open door. The room looked like any other classroom: linoleum floors, bookcases at the back, a blackboard at the front, windows along one side. Ten girls were working in pairs, facing each other, books open on their desks. A young man with a reddish beard and glasses sat at a desk in the front. He was cute but a little geeky. I said, "Hi, I'm Mia."

"C'mon in," he said. "We're studying the *Birkot Hashahar*, page six. You can join a group or work by yourself."

I sat by myself and read over the prayer. I actually knew this one because I had studied it in Toronto. You said the prayer in the morning to thank God for making you a Jew, for making you free. I practiced reading the Hebrew and got a quick lesson from the teacher on pronouncing vowels.

At ten I followed the other girls to the Torah class. The teacher wore leather sandals with kneesocks that disappeared under her long skirt. An enormous pair of plastic-frame glasses swooped down her thin face. An ugly kerchief covered her hair, and a fine mustache fuzzed her upper lip, but she welcomed me so enthusiastically with this crazy Brooklyn accent, I forgot what she looked like. She paired me with a girl named Michelle.

"I'm glad you're here." Michelle opened her book. "I didn't have a *chevruta*."

"A what?"

"A *chevruta*, a study partner."

"Oh, I've never worked with a partner before."

Michelle's face fell a little. "Well, we read together and try and make sense of the text, and then we get together with the class and find out what it really means."

Michelle wore her fair reddish hair pulled back from her thin face in a low ponytail. Her denim skirt was so long it covered the tops of her sandals. I noticed she had sewed up most of the slit in the back, and I wondered how she could walk.

Michelle was from San Francisco. She used to follow the Grateful Dead, until she fell in love with this Jewish guy and followed him to Israel. She was over him now, but she had decided she wanted to become Jewish, so she was undergoing a rigorous Orthodox conversion. She whispered all this to me as if it was top secret.

"Following the Dead must have been so cool."

Michelle frowned. "No, it was soul destroying; it wasn't *Hashem*."

"Oh. I see."

"I just had the strangest sense that I was supposed to be here, like it was my home, you know?"

I nodded even though I didn't know what that felt like. "I used to be really into music too."

"Oh yeah?"

"Yeah, I used to play banjo in a rockabilly band."

Michelle raised her eyebrows. "A what band?"

"Rockabilly. It's like rock and bluegrass mixed together. You know, the Stray Cats, Jerry Lee Lewis." I thought Michelle might say "Cool" or "Wow." Instead she gripped her hands together and looked anxious, so I continued. "I thought I was going to be a musician, but now I know I need to follow a more spiritual path. You know, with God."

Michelle relaxed. "I totally know what you mean." She smoothed the page of her book. "Music is good, but this"—she gestured around us at the studying girls— "this is amazing."

Music was always a huge part of my life. My dad, Don, was a musician who was always on the road. He came and went out of our lives, but his music and instruments stayed in our basement. I grew up listening to his old bluegrass records: the Blue Sky Boys, Bill Monroe and the Carter Family. When I was fifteen, my older brother, Flip, and I formed a rockabilly band, the Neon DayGlos. I spent all of grade ten and eleven playing banjo in seedy bars, dressed like a 1950s pinup. While my school friends were running track and playing in the school orchestra, I was using a fake ID and hanging out with my boyfriend Matt, the bassist for the band.

When I was little, I hoped Don would show up for my birthday parties or track meets, but he never did. My mom, Sheila, said he had his own life to live. I didn't understand why his life didn't include us. When I got older, I realized my mother had never expected Don to stick around. I imagined she'd gotten pregnant "by accident." She never complained about being a single parent, or about Don's absences. Yet I could tell she was thrilled each time he came back.

The spring I was sixteen, Don unexpectedly arrived home mid-tour and locked himself in our basement for a week with a couple of mickeys of vodka. I found out he had been on tour in West Virginia when he discovered his childhood home had been razed to build a Walmart parking lot. His mother had died a few years before and her house had been sold, but Don hadn't realized the beautiful weeping willow in his mother's backyard, as well as all the neighboring gardens, had been paved over by acres of gleaming tarmac. Don was devastated. He abandoned his tour and and came back to the only home he had—our house.

When he finally emerged from the basement, he presented Sheila, Flip and me with the worst song he'd ever written, "Grunge Baby."

You're my little grunge baby,
And I want you to slay me.
Kick me with your Dockers,
You're the sweetest rocker…

The chorus jingled like an advertisement for a furniture warehouse. Don sold the song to a friend putting together a boy band and was able to retire from touring.

I assumed he'd leave after that, but instead he stuck around and slowly became part of our lives. I'd come home from school to find him making spaghetti sauce or fixing the tiling in the bathroom. He helped out with the band and gave me lessons on the banjo. It was like he actually lived at our house. He convinced my mother to sort through the plastic shopping bags of accumulated junk taking over our living room. He even polished my cowboy boots for me.

Then in the spring Don bought a dilapidated cottage up on Lake St. Nora. When the weather turned warm enough, he moved there to fix it up. Sheila, Flip and I joined him for most of August.

In the long hot afternoons, Sheila and Don played old folk songs on the porch while Flip and I raced air mattresses across the cove. In the evenings we ate bean salad, fresh corn on the cob and corned beef sandwiches, and played endless rounds of Hearts. Sometimes we played music together, Sheila and Don on guitars, me on banjo and Flip on improvised pot drums. It was the only summer we didn't spend endless hours driving to catch Don at his summer festival gigs.

All that summer I swam along the shore and looked at the silvery logs in the water—half alive, half dead— and gazed at the peeling bark of the birch trees on the shore. Sometimes I'd walk into the woods and lie down on the forest floor and look up at the towering trees in all their beauty. They were so much older than me, and they'd be there long after I was dead.

Once when I was lying on the forest floor, almost asleep, a breeze wafting over my body, I heard footsteps breaking the twigs. Before I had time to get up, Don was there.

"Oh." I sat up. I tried to brush the twigs and leaves out of my hair. I felt embarrassed to be lying in the dirt.

Don put his hand out. "Don't get up." He crouched awkwardly and then lay beside me with his hands behind his head. I saw him close his eyes and then open them to look up at the sky.

I lay back down. Between the tree branches, clouds sailed across the sky in ever-changing formations. We lay together in silence for a few minutes. Don was so still I thought he'd fallen asleep. Then he murmured, "You could write a song about looking up at the sky through the trees."

"Uh-huh."

Another long pause. "What would you call it?"

I thought about this for a moment. Then I said, "I'd call it 'Catch Your Breath.'"

"Huh."

I turned my head to look at him. "What would you call it?"

Don paused again. "I'd call it 'Catch Your Breath' too."

Michelle was staring at me. I shook my head. Right, I was here to learn. I opened my book. "Let's get started on this Torah thing."

Michelle nodded and we started reading the story of Sarah casting out Hagar. First we read it in English, and then we tried to read the Hebrew. Michelle's Hebrew sucked almost as much as mine, and we didn't get very far. When we took a break, I told Michelle, "I thought Sarah was one of the foremothers. She doesn't sound so great and righteous."

Michelle pursed her lips. "No, she sounds rather human."

"Wouldn't you be pissed if you couldn't get pregnant and your husband took another wife just so he could have a kid?"

Michelle frowned at the text. "That would suck."

"So what's this supposed to mean to us?"

"I don't think we're supposed to study it that way."

"Oh." Well, why bother then? I thought, but it seemed rude to say that, so we just kept reading. The class discussion focused on the interpretations of some guy named Rashi, and on who was righteous and who was not.

At break time we filed into the lounge with students from other classes and drank coffee or tea and snacked on pastries. I looked around for Aviva, but her classes, conducted all in Hebrew, were on another floor. I sat next to Michelle on a saggy orange couch. She gestured with her elbow to a group of giggling girls. "Most of the other students are FFB, and their Hebrew is excellent."

"FF what?"

"FFB. It means *frum*—you know, religious—from birth. They grew up religious and they know all this stuff." Michelle sounded envious. One of the FFB girls came over to us. She had a band of freckles across her snub nose and a long dark braid down her back.

"Are you new here?" she asked me.

"Yes, I'm Mia."

"Hi, I'm Chani." She held out her hand. "We don't really get to know the girls in your classes very well, so you should come Israeli dancing here on Thursday night. It's a blast."

"Oh, is it hard to learn?"

"You'll catch on, no problem." She turned to Michelle. "You should come too."

"Oh, maybe." Michelle twisted her hands behind her.

Chani smiled and went back to her friends.

I turned to Michelle. "She seems really nice. Have you gone dancing?"

"No."

"Why not?"

Michelle lowered her voice. "All they do is talk about *shidduch* dates."

"Is that where you get set up?"

Michelle nodded.

I frowned. "I thought that wasn't until you were older."

"Nope. It starts now."

I felt a twinge in my stomach. I squirmed on the sofa. "You don't want to get married?"

Michelle bit her lip. "No, it's not that. I can't yet." Her voice dropped. "Not until my conversion."

"Oh, well. That's okay." I waved my croissant in the air. "I'm sure they'd understand."

Michelle gripped my arm. "I don't want anyone to know. I just told you because—"

I pulled my arm away from her. "I get it. No worries. When's your exam?"

Michelle sighed. "Only a month to go."

"I'm sure you'll do awesome. Anyway, I'm going to go dancing. It's probably fun, you know, in a wholesome kind of way."

Michelle gave me a funny look.

At 11:30, I followed Michelle into the *halacha* or law class. The students were studying the *Shulchan Aruch* or "The Set Table," a text about keeping kosher. Right away they launched into a discussion about accidentally dropping some milk into a pot of beef stew. Jews weren't supposed to eat milk and meat together. Could the stew be saved or did it have to be thrown out? It was all about proportions. The discussion sounded so ridiculous I thought maybe they were joking, but it was serious. Why couldn't you drain out the bit the milk touched, say *oops* and still praise God?

I was disappointed. I'd hoped the *halacha* class would talk about why we were following the laws. Wasn't that the point of coming to yeshiva—to figure out the Why?

After class I went up to the teacher, Miriam. "I'm wondering if, um, we're going to be discussing the reason behind the laws."

Miriam smiled. "Nope. It's not that kind of class."

"So we're just going to discuss how to interpret the law?"

"Yes, that's right." She smiled again.

I didn't know what else to say, so I nodded and left.

I went downstairs to talk to Rochel.

"So how were your classes? Good?" she asked.

I nodded.

"Great. Are you going to stay for the afternoon or the evening?"

I shook my head. "I think a half day is going to be more than enough." There was no way I could do a full day. I was already exhausted. My head ached from sounding out words and following complex arguments. It was a good ache, but I wanted to collapse upstairs.

Rochel's smile tightened a little. "Most girls who come for the summer want to learn as much as possible. So, go have a rest and come back in the evening. There's Israeli dancing, calligraphy and a course on life-cycle event planning."

I nodded and got up to leave.

"Wait." Rochel put out her hand to stop me. "Are you interested in volunteering?"

"Oh." I stopped. "Yes." *Tikkun olam.* Repairing the world. I could help bring more God to the Earth.

"Old or young people, hospital or school?"

"Um, old people," I decided.

Rochel gave me the pamphlet for an organization called Lifeline for the Old, a craft center for the elderly. "You could also join the Shabbos *mitzvot* group. They give out flowers at Hadassah Hospital."

I took the pamphlets. "I'll think about it," I said.

I spent the rest of the afternoon buying books for my classes and visiting the craft center. I arranged to volunteer two afternoons a week, cutting cloth in the fabric workshop. The coordinator called me Maya and introduced me to a workroom full of old Russian women who looked like they'd pinch my cheeks if I came too close.

I was lying on my bed with my guidebook when Aviva came home. "Hey, how were your classes?" She pulled a bag of Cheezies out of her backpack.

I sat up. "Interesting and exhausting and different. My brain is killing me trying to keep all that new information straight."

"How was the Hebrew level?"

"Oh, I think it'll be okay."

"So." Aviva rested her chin in her palm. "You liked it?"

I thought about the girls in their boring clothes and the *halacha* class and took a big breath. "It's not exactly what I thought it would be like, but yeah, I think it's going to be good."

"I'm so happy for you." Aviva clapped her hands. She looked pleased, as if it were her courses going well. She pointed at my book. "Is that for school?"

"No, it's just a guidebook. I want to go back to the Old City tomorrow and explore. Wanna come?"

"Don't you have classes all day?"

"I finish at one."

"You didn't sign up for a full day?"

"No. Was I supposed to?"

"I just thought you would. You know, with your scholarship and all."

"Oh, there are so many other things I want to do. Volunteer work and tourist stuff, like go up the Mount of Olives, wander through East Jerusalem."

Aviva tugged on her hair. "Oh, I don't think you should do that. It could be really dangerous."

"Oh, c'mon, I'm sure it's fine."

"Look, I don't want to scare you, but you need to be careful." Aviva stood with her hand on the doorknob.

"I will be." I tried to look serious.

"That's good."

"Hey, I was reading about this great hike to an oasis called Ein Gedi." I held up my guidebook. "We could go Friday morning."

"You mean just the two of us?"

"Yeah."

"And hike alone?" Aviva looked at me as if I was crazy.

"Not a good idea?"

"The school offers lots of trips. There's a sign-up sheet in the main lobby. I think there's a night hike at the end of the month."

"Oh, thanks." The end of the month seemed an awfully long time to wait to go hiking.

Aviva went to use the phone in the lobby. She came back a few minutes later. "My mom says hi. She was thrilled to hear you liked your classes."

"Oh, that's great." I looked up from my book. Aviva had already called home to say we'd arrived safely. I hadn't called anyone.

"Doesn't your mom want you to call?"

"She said a postcard would be fine." Sheila was at an art and music festival for most of the summer. I had a phone number for emergencies only.

Aviva didn't know anything about my family except they weren't religious. I was sure she'd never met anyone whose parents weren't married. She didn't know my dad wasn't Jewish or how freaked out my mom had been when I announced I was becoming observant. Sheila had stood in our kitchen and raved for over an hour about the sexist, insular ways of Orthodox Judaism.

"What about your dad?" Aviva looked curious.

"My dad, well, he's away a lot." Aviva looked even more interested. "For business," I lied.

"Oh." Aviva nodded. "Cheezie?" She held out the bag. I helped myself to a handful.

We made pasta salad with olives for dinner and dipped thin sheets of pita in hummus and baba ghanoush. While we ate on the balcony, strange popping noises echoed across the valley. I straightened and tried to peer out into the distance.

"I think that's just a car backfiring," Aviva said.

A few minutes later, more popping noises ricocheted off the building. Aviva tensed. We sat quietly listening. As we were clearing the dishes, another bang resounded, louder and sharper.

"*That* was a gun." Aviva gripped the railing.

"How do you know?"

"Just do."

I stood looking out over the beautiful sand hills.

"Don't worry," Aviva said. "Just stay in the Jewish parts of the city and you'll be fine."

THREE

I closed my eyes and chanted, "I am grateful to you, living King, for restoring my soul to me." I swayed back and forth, my eyes closed so tightly I saw stars. "You are faithful beyond measure." I sang the lines again and looked over the desert. The night's velvet darkness had retreated, taking with it the fleeting dew, leaving the air so dry it felt fiery in my lungs.

Each morning after the mournful cry of the call to prayer jarred me out of sleep, I silently crept out of my sweaty sheets and went up to the rooftop of the B'nos Sarah dorm to gaze out at the pink and yellow panorama of the desert. The morning mist made the sand merge into the sky.

I'd signed up for a school trip to Massada and for a night hike, the way Aviva had suggested, but I really wanted to walk alone down the hill and be surrounded by all that space. I'd never seen a landscape without buildings or trees. I imagined the desert as a vast nothingness, yet I knew it would be different up close. The landscape would flatten and change as I walked. There'd be hills and gullies and wild cacti. From here, the land seemed beautiful, endless and terrifying.

Prayers. I was supposed to be doing my prayers. I turned my back on the desert and forced myself to look at my book.

I'd never felt the need to pray until after that summer up at Don's cottage. At the end of August Sheila, Flip and I went back to Toronto, to work and school and, I'd assumed, the band. Then Flip decided to drop out of university to join the army.

My mom went ballistic. "Don't you know," she yelled, "I sheltered draft dodgers during the Vietnam War?" Of course we knew. Sheila had hidden Don in a barn near Peterborough for months.

Suddenly I had no band, no brother and no boyfriend either. When the Neon DayGlos folded, Matt disappeared. He never returned my messages, and when I went by his apartment, his roommate said he was out. The worst part was I didn't actually miss him; I missed the band.

My life became very lonely. I hadn't joined the school band or the track team because of rehearsing with the Neon DayGlos, so I had few school friends. I tried hanging out at the bars I used to play at. I drank beer and danced with guys with greased-back hair and tattoos. I slept with one of them because I thought it would be fun, except it wasn't. Sex with a stranger was awkward and messy. Then one of the bars got a new bouncer, who confiscated my fake ID, and suddenly I had nowhere to go.

All that fall I kept waiting for Don to come back. By November I realized he was going to live at the cottage year-round. I couldn't understand why he would want to live alone in a shack in the woods, why he didn't want to be with us.

I spent the winter in my room, playing old Carter Family songs: "Keep on the Sunny Side" and "Can the Circle Be Unbroken." I listened to Led Zeppelin and Pink Floyd and my father's old Stanley Brothers records.

I started going for long walks in the frigid night. I'd go down to the boardwalk at the Beaches and let the wind whip snow against my face. I wanted it to sting me out of my lethargy. "Something has to be different," I'd say aloud. Yet nothing changed. My words made my scarf damp, which chapped my chin.

Then one Saturday morning I woke up and the light coming through my curtains had a softer, more translucent quality. I sat up in bed and peered out the window. Thick ice coated the window, the sidewalk, and every house and tree. The maple on our front lawn jingled like wind chimes as the branches moved in the breeze.

The radio said it was minus twenty-five and the roads were like glaciers, but I couldn't wait to get outside. I wanted to skate right down our road and look at the trees dressed up in their shiny winter coats.

After layering on long underwear and snow pants, I crawled down our front stairs. The glare of the sun off the ice made me squint. I inhaled the icy air, drawing the bitterness into my lungs, and watched my breath steam out in smokers' clouds. My exposed cheeks felt stiff in the frigid air. I slid on my bum down our sloped side-walk to the park at the end of the street. A muffled quiet hugged my ears. No people or traffic, just the sound of the branches tinkling in the wind, and the occasional loud crack as limbs snapped under the weight of the ice.

My boots made a satisfying crunch as they sank through the top layer of brittle snow covering the park. I lay on the end of the kids' slide, looking up at the bright blue sky wisped with clouds. It made me think of the afternoon I lay in the clearing with Don. Today the trees looked like silver lace. The branches sounded like thousands of crystal wineglasses being tapped by silver spoons. If only the world was always this frozen, I thought, and I could stay looking at the trees forever.

❧

I'd come a long way since that miserable winter. Now I had God, the yeshiva girls and the desert to get to know.

With them, I'd never be lonely. I quickly finished the last prayer and headed down to meet Michelle for class.

Although my yeshiva courses were different than I expected, I was gradually adapting. I'd started to appreciate the textual analysis. Each word in the Torah was open to scrutiny. What did it mean and how was it used? How had it been interpreted through the centuries? I liked the prayer and biblical Hebrew classes best. Each new word I learned unlocked part of the puzzle. I quickly memorized new vocabulary so I could feel the tiny thrill of recognizing a word as I chanted it aloud.

The only class I couldn't get into was the *halacha*, the law class. We'd moved on to a discussion of whether meat and milk could touch in a refrigerator. We'd had the same discussion yesterday. And, I swear, the day before that. The answer was yes, because they were cold. But if they were hot, well, that was a different story. I couldn't believe we were discussing this. Who cared? The previous week we'd studied how many hours you had to wait between eating meat and milk. The other students seemed riveted by the geographical differences: most Europeans waited six hours, except for the Dutch, who only waited one. As the week progressed, my frustration with the class intensified. Why, oh why, couldn't we discuss *why* God said not to eat meat and milk together? Was it human rights? Animal rights? Indigestion?

I sighed and rested my head on my notebook. Maybe I could sign up for a class more focused on God, or on how to bring more spirituality into the world.

After *halacha* class all the students piled through the double doors of the *beit midrash*, the main study hall, and found places for the midday prayers. It was a short service, mostly prayed individually. At the end, we all sang the closing prayer together. I felt a glow of satisfaction within me. Voices rose around me, true in their devotion. Each girl loved *Hashem* and wanted to make His world a better place. I nodded to myself. I just needed everything I did at B'nos Sarah to feel like this.

When prayers were finished, I headed down to Rochel's office and sat in the hard-backed chair in front of her desk. "I'm wondering if I can take another class instead of *halacha*."

Rochel peered at me over her reading glasses. I looked back at her as earnestly as I could. She pulled out my student card and glanced at my courses. "No, not at your level. You have to have the building blocks, a foundation of the laws, first, and of course a higher level of Hebrew."

"Oh." I exhaled a breath I didn't know I was holding. "Are there any courses on why we should be Jewish?"

Rochel furrowed her brow. "Why we should be Jewish?"

"You know." I knit my fingers together behind my back. "Spiritual discussions of why we keep kosher, or about God."

Rochel looked confused. I imagined her thinking, *It's always these ba'al teshuvah*, these newly religious girls, who ask these things. She shook her head. "You should attend our Shabbos retreats. They discuss more personal matters." She pulled out a flyer. "There's one this weekend. It's sponsored by the Cohen Foundation and it's very reasonably priced. I think you'd enjoy the guest speaker."

I thanked her and took the flyer. On the cover was a picture of a hotel in a grove of trees under the words *Join us for a spiritual retreat*. Most of the sessions had hokey titles like *God and You, forging a bond*, but it also looked restful. I had some spending money left over from a waitressing job and from my grad present from my mom's mother, Bubbie Bess. Maybe Aviva and I could go together.

After class I took the bus to the Old City. Most afternoons I volunteered at the craft center or explored the city. I'd tried to find someone to explore Jerusalem with, but most of the other girls had signed up for a full-day program. So I went back on my own to the Hurva Synagogue and the Roman ruins of the Cardo. I wandered through the Jewish quarter's restored alleys and expensive shops. In the Armenian quarter I sat in the beautiful cathedral Aviva had wrinkled her nose at.

Outside the Old City I walked through different neigh-borhoods, explored museums and hung out in Liberty Bell Park, with its grove of olive trees. I felt so proud to be a Jew, to explore my beautiful country and know that it had all been built in less than fifty years.

Each time I went to the Old City, I visited the *Kotel*. I decided I had to develop a connection with the wall. I hadn't grown up thinking it was special, so how could I form an instant bond?

And so I stood at the wall and let my head rest against the hot stones. I'd wait for a tour group to squeeze their notes into the wall's crevices, and then I'd chant from my prayer book as fast as I could, so the women waiting behind me could have their turn. I felt empty, like a prayer machine. The *Kotel* was too crowded for God. If God was anywhere, He was in that vast desert space surrounding the city.

At the school library I'd read up on the *Kotel's* history. The high priests had made their offerings and spoken with God there. Centuries of exiled Jews dreamed of it from Russian *shtetls* and Moroccan *mellahs*. But when I stood with my body pressed to those warm stones I thought, What if it's just a stone wall, or worse, what if all the rabbis were wrong and it's just a retaining wall pilgrims used to piss on? This is an important Jewish symbol, I reminded myself, a spiritual holy place. The word *icon* lingered in my mind. I had learned a story about honoring false gods and praying before idols.

What was the difference between praying to God in front of the wall or on your own? Was the wall really, truly holy or was it holy because people decided it was? Was there a difference?

I gave the *Kotel* a parting tap and sighed. I'd wanted to let Israel fill me up. It was, but slowly. What if I'd gone to Ireland, where Don's ancestors were from, and decided the coastal towns were my spiritual homeland? Could I have as easily become a Catholic as a Jew?

I climbed the stairs to the balcony overlooking the Temple Mount. The Dome glimmered like a gold-wrapped chocolate in a forbidden box. All the other times I came, the complex had been empty, but today people were lined up in neat rows. Could I go in too? I'd never imagined it was open to tourists. A shiver ran down my spine. I could be near those colors—heavenly blue and glimmering gold. I trotted down the stairs and back across the plaza toward an exit near the men's side. After studying my guidebook, I made a few wrong turns through dark alleys until I came to a tunnel with a metal gate and a guard. On the other side, a corridor of trees led toward the Dome. Green. I stared at the row of trees, the color a relief to my eyes. Forget the Dome. I wanted to go and sit under those trees.

The guard eyed me warily.

"Can I go in?"

He shook his head and pointed to a sign on the wall listing the hours of operation. "Now it's prayers."

I studied the sign. I'd have to come another day.

From the Old City I wandered up to Ben Yehuda Street, a pedestrian road lined with shops and cafés. Tourists perused jewelry, T-shirts, menorahs and candlesticks. Israelis drinking strong coffee filled the cafés. At the foot of the street, soldiers with M16s hung out at Zion Square. They looked even younger than me.

Before I left for Israel, Sheila had given me two envelopes of money. "This one is for you and this one is for helping others. Just don't give the money to some cult that thinks they're going to bring the Messiah."

That was so my mom. Sheila worked with at-risk teens and she was also a peace activist. I had attended rallies and helped her canvass until I was thirteen. After that I was more interested in learning to play Don's instruments, especially the banjo.

Sheila had also given me two envelopes of money when I went to visit my cousin Emily in New York the year before. I bought loaves of bread, cheese, carrots and juice boxes and made thirty-five lunches. I distributed them in Penn Station in half an hour. People took my lunches; a few older people said, "Bless you, child."

Now, before yeshiva started for the day, I'd filled pitas with hummus, cucumber and tomato. As I walked up Ben Yehuda Street, I gave a sandwich to an old Russian man putting on a show with two shabby marionettes, and one to a young guy who played the flute badly. Midway up the street I gave a sandwich to a very old woman sitting on a carpet holding an empty margarine tub. When I put a sandwich in front of a kid doing magic tricks, he called after me, "Lady, I need money, not food." I tucked my head between my shoulders and beetled up Ben Yehuda.

At first I was a little freaked out by the homeless people. How could there be beggars in Israel? Didn't the state take care of its people? No, I decided, it was like home. People fell through the cracks, even if everyone was Jewish. Not only were the doctors, teachers and bus drivers Jewish, but so were the prostitutes and beggars.

On the way up to the bus stop I stopped to listen to a guy playing the guitar. He stood near King George Street, within earshot of the crowds gathered to wait for the number 4 bus to Mount Scopus, or the 9 to Givat Ram. He had a thin, muscular build, short tousled brown hair and a sharp jaw line. A large pair of aviator sunglasses obscured his eyes. I guessed he was American, in his twenties. I stood for a moment, listening to him play "California Dreamin'." He had an okay voice, nothing spectacular.

I was about to leave when he started strumming Patsy Cline's "Crazy." I stood with my hands on my hips. My mom has a thing for old-time country singers like Patsy, and I'd grown up listening to a lot of that kind of music. Pedestrians shuffled by, some stopping to listen. I peeked through the crowd to get a better look. Despite the heat, the guitarist wore jeans slung low around narrow hips;

his leather belt had a cowboy buckle. On his feet was a beat-up pair of Converse sneakers. His open guitar case held loose change.

As his voice soared on the chorus, he let his sunglasses slide down his nose. He winked at a young girl and she dissolved in giggles. I couldn't help smiling. Would he sing "Stand by Your Man" next? I found myself singing along as I checked out his lithe forearms. I'd always had a thing for sexy arms. Before I left, I weaved through the other listeners and dropped the last sandwich into his guitar case with the shekels he'd collected. He nodded at me, and I smiled back.

Before getting on my bus, I wandered down a side street to browse in a bookstore. When I came out, the guitar player was sitting on a bench, tuning his strings.

"Hey," he said.

I kept walking.

"Hey, you, sandwich girl." I whirled around. The guitar player held out the sandwich. "You didn't have to."

"Oh." I took the pita from his outstretched hand.

"I mean, thanks and all. I'm sure it's very good. I just don't need it." He squinted over the top of his sunglasses, one eyebrow rising toward his hairline. His eyes were an unusually clear turquoise, like the water in a swimming pool.

"You're welcome." I grasped the sandwich behind me, my cheeks burning. He wasn't just looking at me; he was making the kind of eye contact guys make when they want you to feel you are the only girl in the world.

"I thought maybe you were hungry." I rubbed one calf against the other. He looked amused, his head tilted to the side, as if waiting for me to say something else. I swallowed. "I should get going."

"Wait, I have a song for you." He had a mischievous smile.

"I..."

"It'll just be a second."

"I have to go." I hurried to the bus stop and boarded my bus. I hung on to a seat and tried to calm my racing pulse.

The old Mia would have been thrilled if a guy wanted to sing her a song. I'd have flirted, grabbed the guitar and composed a little three-chord ditty about a busker who sang old country songs. And the new Mia? I wasn't supposed to hang out with guys—that was part of being religious. When you were ready to get married, a go-between set you up with someone compatible and you went on a series of dates to determine if he was your *b'shert*—"the one." You didn't even shake hands or touch until after you got married.

The bus sharply rounded a corner, and I grabbed the seat to avoid falling. Why did the guitar guy have a song for me? I was wearing a long skirt and a dorky sunhat. My life was about good works and spirituality, not appearances.

Shit. I was still finding cute guys, or they were finding me. I should lock myself up in the B'nos Sarah dormitory.

I decided not to give out any more sandwiches; it was embarrassing. The rest of Sheila's money could go to B'nos Sarah or the craft center. Or I'd drop it into the old woman's margarine tub.

Back at the dorm I put on my exercise pants and a baggy T-shirt, slid my Madonna CD into my Discman and fast-forwarded to "Holiday." I'd been a Madonna fan ever since I heard the *Like a Virgin* album when I was ten.

Running in Israel was an obstacle course of steep hills and amazing views. On my route up to Mount Scopus I first waged the grueling uphill battle to Hebrew University. I could feel my glutes and hamstrings bunch and tighten. Blood pounded in my head as my labored breath filled me. I wasn't Mia Quinn; I was a body winning a race, pushing itself up a hill. I was a conqueror of sand and Jerusalem stone, my pulse surging to new highs. My heart pumped, muscles flexed, bones strode on a swell of endorphins. The tightness from sitting on a hard wooden chair and squinting at Hebrew texts dissolved as I pumped my arms up the hill. Sweat trickled down my forehead, pooled in my bra, dampened my hair.

At the top of the hill the magnificent vista of Jerusalem came into view as I cruised the relatively flat road around the Mormon College campus. Then I endured the knee-jarring downhill plunge past the falafel stand that doubled as a dentist's office. I ignored the old men who leered each time I passed. The road bottomed out by the Hyatt Hotel and then rose again up to French Hill, the steepest part of the whole run. A shortcut through the Hadassah Hospital parking lot and up a vacant hill made the final surge a little shorter, yet also steeper. I could only make it if I sprinted and timed it to correspond with Madonna's "Rescue Me."

I used the edge of my T-shirt to wipe the sweat out of my eyes as I turned in to the parking lot. Only a few more moments of torture. "Rescue Me" came on, the pulse of the drums, the clear vocals helping me pick up my pace.

I started working toward my sprint, my feet pounding the cracked pavement. The sun glared off the car windows. Heat seemed to be emanating from me, yet my arms kept pummeling the air. A car full of young guys honked at me and gave a cheer. I pretended not to see them.

Finally I passed through the metal gate to the field. Less than a minute now. My heart surged, firing my legs up the dry dusty path. The crest was only strides away. *Rescue me.* I went over the top and started leaping like a ballet dancer with my arms wide in a grand jeté.

Then I saw a boy on a donkey coming up the hill toward me. My euphoric high became a surge of panic. I jumped out of the way, into the field of dry grass. Staggering,

I braked hard and stared at the boy as he passed. "Shalom," I whispered. He stared back at me as he trotted by.

I struggled to catch my breath. What was an Arab kid on a donkey doing in the middle of French Hill? Then I saw the goats following him. I imagined him thinking, Why is some crazy girl running through the field?

I shook my head and continued running uphill through the curving streets of tidy French Hill apartments. At the lookout, I sucked ferociously on my water bottle, wiped the sweat dripping down my face and cursed my modest exercise pants. I took off my Discman and lifted one leg onto the park bench to stretch out my taut, pinging hamstrings. Sometimes I fantasized about the slinky purple one-piece exercise suit I used to wear when I jogged at home. No one had glanced twice at me. Well, almost no one, except for some pervy old men and drooling adolescent boys. Here there'd be traffic accidents.

When I got back to the dorm, Aviva was sitting cross-legged on her bed with a cheap Yamaha guitar.

"Hey, where did you get that?" I asked.

"Oh, one of the girls from my class lent it to me. You were running again?"

"Yeah." I took a swig of water.

"Isn't it crazy hot?"

"I'm starting to get used to it." I sat down on the floor to stretch.

"You know, there's a women's gym some of the girls belong to."

"I'm not much of a gym person. Besides, this way I get to see more of the city. Hey, I didn't know you played guitar."

Aviva looked like she might say something else about my running. Then she looked down at the guitar. "I'm trying to teach myself so I can play for *havdalah*."

"What's *havdalah*?"

"You know, the prayers you sing at the end of Shabbos."

"Oh, right." I wiped my hands on my baggy T-shirt and reached for the guitar. "Let me tune it for you."

Aviva handed it over. "I didn't know you could play." She gawked as I adjusted the strings. "You can do that without one of those tuners?"

I nodded and started strumming "Stairway to Heaven." "How does that *hava*-whatever song go?"

Aviva hummed and I started playing along.

Aviva's mouth dropped open. "You can just play what I sing?"

"Sure. You put fingers like this and then—"

"Hey, could you play for choir?"

"Um, sure. That would be fun." I hadn't thought about playing Jewish music. Guitars and playing for other people were part of my old life.

"How about this? Can you play this?" She sang another tune, and I played along. Aviva gaped at me. "How do you do that?"

"I just hear it. My dad taught me. He's a—I mean, he's good at music."

"Wow, wait till the other girls hear." Aviva looked ready to run down the hall and call them into our room right then.

I handed back the guitar and then wished I hadn't. "How long do you have the guitar for?"

"Oh, just a few hours." She concentrated on playing a G chord.

I leaned over and adjusted her fingers.

"Like that?" She played the chord.

"Yeah, that's right." I sat back on my bed. "Hey, have you ever been to the Dome of the Rock?"

Aviva looked up from the guitar. "No."

"Do you wanna come with me? We could go Friday."

Aviva looked mortified. "Don't you know? Jews shouldn't go there."

"Let me guess." I flopped back on my bed. "It's not safe."

Aviva put down the guitar. "Mia, you could be walking right over the *Ir Hakodesh,* the holiest part of the temple, and not know it." Her eyes stretched wide to show how serious she was.

"Huh, I never thought of that." I guessed the *ir ha-*whatever was the inner sanctum. I sat up and started stretching my calves. "So, to rebuild the temple, it would have to be where the Dome is?"

"Uh-huh."

"Wooo-eeee. You'd have to destroy the dome, huh?"

"Yes. That's one reason why Palestinians want control of Jerusalem."

"You can't blame them."

"My father says they should have settled for what the UN offered in '48."

"What was that?"

"The UN wanted to make Israel into two states, one Jewish and one Palestinian. The Jews agreed, although reluctantly. The Palestinians refused and started the war."

"I guess they were determined to keep their homeland."

A flash of contempt glinted in Aviva's eyes. "Too bad they couldn't compromise just a little. They could have had half of Jerusalem. Lucky for us though."

I looked at Aviva for a moment and thought about the boy and his goats. "Yep, lucky for us." I got up to shower.

FOUR

I decided to skip *halacha* class the next afternoon. I didn't feel like going to the Old City or the craft center, so I wandered down Ben Yehuda again. I bought a stack of postcards and sat on a shady patio sipping coffee and trying to write to Sheila. *Dear Mom, Israel is really hot. Dear Mom, School is everything I thought it would be.* I decided on *Dear Mom, Israel is a very interesting and spiritual place.*

I became religious because I'd decided I needed more spirituality in my life. The day last winter when I lay in the snow during the ice storm and looked up at the trees, I'd had a sense of how awesome the world was. I felt myself soar up with those trees, and I knew I wanted more moments like that. I just didn't know how to get them. I had trekked back to the park a few days after the storm, but the ice had melted and cracked the branches into odd, truncated shapes. The winter felt old and shabby. It made me dizzy to stare up at the sky.

My life back then felt very gray. With Don, Flip and the band gone, depression settled on me like a weight on my chest. Everything I did felt pointless. My school friends were excited about going to university or traveling after grad, but I had no idea what I wanted to do or be. I'd always thought I'd be a musician, but now I wasn't sure. I didn't want to be like Don, always away on tour, always wandering.

One day I was in my favorite café when a small poster with a picture of a menorah on it caught my eye.

Spiritually Exhausted?
Come renew your Jewish soul through song.
Celebrate Shabbat in our community.

It was sponsored by a group called Jewish Outreach. I read the poster again. I liked to sing, and I felt spiritually exhausted, empty even. I knew a little bit about Judaism from my Bubbie Bess. We used to have Friday-night dinners at her house when I was younger. Bess always lit Shabbat candles and said a prayer over the wine. I stood in the café staring up at the bulletin board and thought about those dinners at Bess's house, how peaceful they had felt. I wrote down the Jewish Outreach number and stuck it in my pocket.

I spent the week hemming and hawing about calling. Finally I dared myself to call. I figured I didn't have to go if it sounded too weird. When I called, I spoke to a Mr. Zev Teitelbaum.

"Hi, I saw your poster about Shabbat, and I was thinking I might like to try it."

"Of course you can come for Shabbos. Every week if you like."

"Oh, well, maybe just once would be okay. I'm not really all that Jewish. I mean, my mom is, but I don't really know anything and—"

"So, you'll come and learn. This Friday, okay?"

"Well, okay."

"You should go to the Blumes' house. They live at— do you have a pen?"

"Um, sure. This is at someone's house?"

"Yes. You should have Shabbos in the community."

"Oh. Should I bring something?"

"No, just come."

He gave me the address and told me to wear a long skirt—nothing skimpy—which made me feel both embarrassed and nervous.

I almost didn't go. I stood in front of the mirror at home trying to decide between a knee-length velvet circle skirt and a longer tube skirt. The circle skirt showed off my long legs and the tube skirt was fitted across the butt. Neither were appropriate. In the end I wore the circle skirt with my favorite pair of cowboy boots and an almost modest cardigan with beading across the chest. The directions were to a neighborhood where a lot of Orthodox Jews lived. When I rang the bell, a huge bearded guy in a *kippah* answered the door like he'd been waiting all his life for me to show up.

"Welcome, welcome. I'm Joseph Blume. Please come in." He took my coat. "Have you ever been for Shabbos before?"

I shook my head. I'd been to my bubbie's, but never to an Orthodox home. I wanted to back out the door.

He clasped his hands together. "Such an honor to share your first Shabbos with you." He sounded genuinely excited. "Chava," he called down the hallway to the kitchen, "this is Mia's first Shabbos!"

Mrs. Blume, a little mousey thing wearing an awful gray hat, came down the hall. She looked like a small mushroom. She gave me a huge smile and grabbed my hands. "We're so happy you could come." I kept nodding and smiling.

I followed the Blumes into a dining room crowded with people standing around a table laid with a white cloth and blue-edged china. Mr. Blume invited everyone to sit down, and a teenage girl with dark curly hair, the Blumes' daughter I guessed, came in from the kitchen.

Mrs. Blume blessed the candles. I remembered some of the words from Bubbie Bess's house and mumbled along.

A sense of nostalgia for Bess and her apartment enveloped me.

Then Mr. Blume sang a Hebrew love song about a woman of valor. I watched in awe as this fat middle-aged man sang this loving song to his frumpy wife in front of a table of guests. I tried to picture Don singing Sheila a love song in front of our family. Even though he was a musician and had a beautiful voice, I couldn't imagine it. I felt a lump in my throat like I was going to cry. I swallowed it away.

After the song, Mr. Blume's daughter, Aviva, stood before him and he put his hands on her head and whispered a blessing in her ear. I'd never seen that before and I started to tear up. I wanted to get up and excuse myself to go to the bathroom, but the table was so crowded, at least six people would have had to move to let me out. So I sniffed a little and murmured "Allergies" and let my hair fall in front of my face, just in case anyone was looking at me. They weren't. They were all watching this dad show how much he loved his daughter. I tried to imagine Don giving me any kind of blessing, or even a song—it *so* wasn't going to happen. I gritted my teeth.

What if I made my future different? What if that was me at one end of the table with a husband who sang me love songs every Friday night even though we'd been married twenty years? What if I had a husband who loved our children to pieces and blessed them every week with a secret whisper in their ears? What if?

THE BOOK OF TREES

Mr. Blume blessed the wine and then everyone filed
into the kitchen to wash their hands in a complicated ritual
I didn't understand, pouring water over each hand with
a special pitcher. All the guests filed back to the table and
sat silently until Mr. Blume blessed the *challah*, a braided
bread, and passed it around. I'd never sat in silence with
a room of people before, not even for a minute.

After the meal, the Blumes passed around little
song-books. I watched as Mr. Blume closed his eyes,
tipped back his head and sang *"Ribbono shel Olam."*
"Master of the Universe." His family joined him, their
voices floating on the wide-open notes. The other guests
joined in as best they could, stumbling through the
transliteration.

I started to sing the song too, and an amazing
feeling rose inside me. As I sang, I could feel our voices
bringing peace into the world. I wanted to hug each
person at the table because I felt happy and oddly
united with these strangers. I wanted to feel this way—
connected to others—all the time.

I went home elated, humming one of the songs on
the subway. At the Blumes', all the pieces seemed to fit
together. They worked all week and then they rested and
celebrated the Sabbath together, sharing what they had
with others. They sang songs at the end of the meal, with
their eyes closed, and a feeling of godliness filled the room.
It was better than playing with the band. It wasn't just
music, it was spiritual music. And the Blumes didn't even

need alcohol or a joint to have a good time. Singing at that religious dinner was like being in the frozen trees, except you didn't have to wait for an ice storm. Every Friday you could be with friends and family and make that feeling through song, and you could even name that feeling: *God*. I couldn't wait to call Zev Teitelbaum.

"I want to come to another dinner, and I want to learn more," I told him. "I want to learn about God."

"Wonderful," he said.

I started going back to the park at the end of the street in the evenings. It was spring by then and the trees were starting to bud. Each new shoot made me feel like the world was changing, and I was part of it. I'd lie on the slide and look up at the trees. I wasn't exactly sure how to define God, but when I saw those trees, I felt sure God and nature were the same thing. I also felt you could create God's presence with beautiful music. I never discussed this with Aviva or her family or at my classes. It felt too personal.

Suddenly all my actions had a purpose: to bring more God into the world. Instead of trying to be the coolest or sexiest girl, or the best musician, I could help others by following God's commandments: love your neighbor, honor your mother and father. This, in turn, would bring peace to myself and others. God, peace, music, nature—it all seemed to form a beautiful cloud of happiness in my head.

Despite my religious conversion, I had some trouble with the bit about honoring my mother and father. I was still angry with Don. He hadn't called all winter. He sent me a postcard, but all it said was *Enjoying the snow and ice. How's the band? Don.*

Not even "Love, Don." I never wrote back.

I finished my coffee, stuck my unfinished postcard in my backpack and headed up to the bus stop. On the way up the street I saw the guitar player sitting on a bench picking coins out of his case. I ducked my head and tried to scurry past, but he gazed right at me and called out, "Hey."

"Oh, hi."

He stood with his legs wide, one hip cocked forward, wearing an olive green Che Guevara T-shirt, his jeans resting low on his hips. His body was compact and muscular in a sinewy way. His legs were long and he was taller than me.

"I hope I didn't insult you the other day. I'm sure your sandwich was great. I just didn't want you to think..."

"It's okay."

"Anyway, I wanted to play you something." He gave me a cocky smile.

"Oh…"

"Just wait, okay?" He picked up his guitar and sang.

Sandwiches are beautiful, sandwiches are fine,
I like sandwiches, I eat them all the time.
I eat them for my breakfast and I eat them for my lunch,
If I had a hundred sandwiches, I'd eat them all at once.

I burst out laughing. I let my body hunch forward, arms dangling. The tension in my neck melted away.

He grinned at me. "You know that song?"

"My dad used to sing it to me."

He laughed and took off his sunglasses. Again I was surprised by his light, clear eyes. "I'm Andrew." He stretched out his hand.

"Mia. I'm sorry, I don't shake hands." I waved at him.

"Germ fetish?"

I shrugged. "I'm just not into it."

He raised one eyebrow.

"I'm religious."

"Yeah, so. I'm a Sagittarius." He bent to scoop more change out of his guitar case.

"I think my bus is coming."

"I'm heading to the Russian Compound for a drink." He put his guitar in the case and picked it up. "Coming?"

"I…"

"You look thirsty. C'mon."

He started strolling down the street. He had a casual, relaxed stride, like nothing bothered him. I followed him because he was still talking.

"So your dad is a musician?"

I had to run a few steps to catch up. What if someone walked by and saw me? "Yes, a songwriter too. You know the band the Jaywalkers?"

He stopped short, and I almost bumped into him. "That lame boy band?"

"My dad sold a song to the people who put the band together."

"Ouch."

"Yeah, well, he was sick of driving the folk-music circuit, and selling the song gave him enough to retire."

"Sweet." He nodded and continued down the street.

I had a sudden urge to ask Andrew if I could borrow his guitar and play him Don's tree song. "My father's other songs are very beautiful. There's one about a tree."

"You should play one for me."

"I'm more into banjo."

His eyes widened. "Unusual choice."

"My dad bought one for me. He gave my brother Flip a mandolin."

"What are you guys, the Partridge Family?" He flashed me a smile, and the corners of his eyes crinkled up. I couldn't help smiling back.

We crossed King David Street and headed up the hill into the Russian Compound, an area of bars and cafés surrounding a large Russian Orthodox Church.

Andrew gestured toward some seats outside a bar.

"Do you mind if we sit inside, out of the sun?" I didn't want anyone from school to see me at a bar. With a guy.

He shrugged and we went inside. He sat loose and relaxed: legs spread, hips tilted, thumbs casually hooked through the belt loops of his jeans. Out of the glare I studied him. He had a thin, angular face. I could tell he'd broken his nose, maybe more than once. He wore one small stud in his ear, and I could see the scar from an old eyebrow ring.

I felt my forehead muscles ease. I hadn't been in a bar like this—dim, wooden tables, black graffiti-covered walls—since I had become religious. When Don didn't come back from his cottage, I'd shoved my banjo and guitar in the basement and given up playing.

We sat at a scratched wooden table, and I studied the band posters. I wanted to shake out my hair, run my fingers through it, maybe lean one elbow on the table and prop up my chin.

A waitress with dyed blond hair and too-tight jeans eyed me from behind her thick-rimmed glasses as she took my order for lemonade. Andrew ordered a beer, and I wished I had done the same. I could almost taste the sweet bitter liquid.

"So, the banjo, huh?"

I nodded. "My dad has this thing about the South, old-timey stuff. He's from West Virginia."

"You're not from there."

"No," I laughed. "Toronto. You?"

"Portland. More recently this beach on the Oregon coast. So you're giving out sandwiches. That's what you do."

"One thing." I laughed self-consciously.

"It's a good thing."

"I'm here studying at a yeshiva—that's a Jewish seminary—to learn Torah."

The waitress brought our drinks. I drained mine and stirred the ice with a straw.

Andrew leaned back in his chair, looking intently at me. "Sounds interesting."

"Some of it is."

"And the rest?"

I sighed and leaned back in my chair, fiddled with my straw. "It's very fragmented and detail-oriented. I'm more of a big-picture person." Again I wanted to play with my hair, prop my feet on the rungs of Andrew's chair.

"So stop going."

"Oh, I'm sure it'll get better." A giggle rose up my throat. "I'm…"

He leaned forward, resting his crossed arms on the table. "You're what?"

"I'm playing hooky right now."

"Huh," he drawled, "aren't you a crazy girl."

We both started to laugh. I signaled for the waitress and ordered a beer.

By four o'clock I'd learned Andrew had been traveling through Turkey when he became friends with this Dutch guy who suggested they take a boat to Israel. He'd been here three months. He busked afternoons, did a few shifts moving stuff at the Israel Art Museum and lived in a hostel near Zion Gate in the Old City. He had no siblings, and his mother, the only relative he mentioned, lived in Portland. Before traveling, he'd worked in a lab doing drug trials. He liked to surf.

"Why busking?" I asked.

"Why not? You could join me, teach me some bluegrass. We'll be a duo."

"You strike me as more rock 'n' roll."

"I could learn." He gave me an intense, piercing look.

I drummed my fingers on the table and looked away. "So, how long will you stay?"

He shrugged. "Until it's time to move on. You should come by the hostel. There's always someone in the late afternoons with a guitar or bongo drums."

I almost said *No, I can't*, or *Religious girls don't*. I nodded instead and got up to leave. "I'm sure I'll see you around."

FIVE

On Friday morning I went to the *shuk*, the outdoor market, to buy some fruit and snacks for the week. On the way home I strolled down Ben Yehuda Street to see if Andrew was playing. He wasn't at his usual spot. I stood by the bench and tapped my sandal on the pavement. He hadn't been there since our drink in the bar earlier in the week. Not that I'd been looking. I'd just glanced up and down the pedestrian walkway. Oh, and once I'd wandered back up to the Russian Compound and looked in the bars.

I checked my watch. I needed to get back to B'nos Sarah to catch the bus for the Shabbos retreat.

Air-conditioning tinged with body odor blasted my face as I boarded the bus. I chose a seat near the front to minimize the bouncing as the bus turned corners.

Soldiers with guns across their backs crowded the aisle. I closed my eyes for a second and took a few deep breaths.

Something hard knocked at my temple. I brushed it aside and turned to look. The butt end of a soldier's M16 tapped my head. I froze, a small *"aah"* escaping my lips. The soldier turned, saw me and said, *"Slicha"*—Sorry— and repositioned his gun. I started breathing again. He said something in Hebrew and laughed. I laughed too, even though I had no idea what he was saying. He had big, caramel-colored eyes and a stubbly chin. I felt his eyes rake over me, and I blushed from my cleft chin to my widow's peak.

This wasn't the first time I'd noticed guys openly checking me out. The clerk at my favorite coffee shop on Emek Refaim purposely flexed as he brewed my latte. The falafel guy near the bus stop on King George winked and smiled at me. Even the bus driver last week, a young guy with a dimple in his chin and a sexy pair of sunglasses, looked me up and down when I got on the bus. "Don't ring the bell for nothing," he chastised a group of giggling pre-teen girls. *"Slicha,"* they called back. "Yeah, yeah," he said. But when I asked him, in English, where to get off for the Islamic Museum, he grinned. "So polite! I'll drop you right in front."

I didn't get it. I always wore long, modest skirts and three-quarter-length-sleeve tops. My best features, my long legs, were always covered up. I wasn't beautiful.

I had classic Quinn family features: a too-long face and a too-high forehead.

Aviva was talking to her mom on the lounge phone when I got home. I gave her a sweaty wave as I passed by. Aviva said goodbye and followed me into our room. "Hey, I was wondering what happened to you."

"The *shuk* was really busy." I didn't mention my side trip down Ben Yehuda.

"Did you get the fruit?"

"Yep, and some pastries." I stacked the bags next to our tiny bar fridge and then sat down on my bed and drank a big glass of water. "Can I ask you something?"

"Sure."

I took a deep breath. "Do you think I'm modest?"

"Sure." Aviva giggled.

"What?"

"Nothing."

"What?" I slapped a hand against my knee.

"Well, you do have a kind of sexy walk."

I stamped my foot. "Damn, I knew it."

Aviva giggled some more.

"How can I change that?"

Aviva shrugged. "The girls are all jealous. No one can figure out how you move. Even Rabbi Simon notices but pretends he doesn't."

I sighed. It was worse than I'd thought. "I'll have to learn to move differently." I stood up and tried to walk as woodenly as possible. "Better?"

Aviva laughed, so I pretended to be a robot.

Aviva sat up. "Actually, can I tell you something?"

"Sure."

Aviva took a little breath. "It's also the way you dress."

"Oh." I looked down at my cherry-print skirt.

"It draws attention to you."

"That's bad?"

"Well...yes."

"I see." I didn't really know what to say. Maybe if I dressed in bland skirts and pastel T-shirts like all the other girls, Andrew wouldn't have looked twice at me.

Aviva got up. "You only have twenty minutes until the bus leaves for the retreat. I'm going to wait in the lounge."

"Okay. I won't be long."

Aviva put her hand on my arm. "I hope I didn't make you feel bad."

"No, it's okay. It's good to know. I want to be, you know, modest."

"You'll still be sexy with that hair." She tugged a curl hanging down my back

After my shower I stood in front of the mirror. My cheeks were still red from the heat. I shook out my damp hair and ran a comb through it. It was the same rich auburn as my Aunt Therese's hair. I was growing out my long bangs and usually wore my hair loose, the layers framing my face. Enough with that. I carefully wove my hair into two tight French braids and pulled the ends around my head in a crown. It looked corny, but my neck would feel cooler and no one could accuse me of having sexy hair. I quickly pulled on a plain skirt and my most modest black top. Suddenly I looked like everyone else at B'nos Sarah. A little shiver of terror made my arm hairs stand up. I wanted to rip off the skirt and put on my polka-dot pencil skirt, or the leopard-print dress I'd left at home. I didn't bring it because the sweetheart neckline exposed the little rose tattoo below my collarbone.

Aviva knocked on the door, then stuck her head in. "Are you ready? Hey, you look nice."

"You think?"

"Yes, really. Let's go or we'll miss the bus." She was holding the door, so I grabbed my backpack and followed her outside.

After we passed the outskirts of Jerusalem, with its white houses perched on cliffs, the bus descended a steep hill into a barren brown valley. My ears popped with the change in elevation. We were heading west into the Judean Desert. I stared out the window. I'd expected flat open spaces, not these rocky hills. They made me feel claustrophobic. I put my head back against the seat and closed my eyes. Twenty minutes later I was fantasizing about a summer rain when the bus started climbing through a forested area. Small Mediterranean pines stood in neat rows, spiraling up the hills. I pressed a hand against the window and stared at the trees. There was something weird about the forest. No undergrowth or bushes, not even weeds, grew between the neatly spaced trees.

The bus arrived at the top of the mountain and stopped by a plain two-story building. We filed through a courtyard and into a sun-filled stucco lobby with low, cheaply upholstered sofas and potted plants. Aviva and I checked in and took our bags up to our room. I laid out my blouse so it wouldn't wrinkle. There was no TV, just two low white beds and a table with two upright chairs. Aviva went to fill the ice bucket and look for a drink machine to stock up on Diet Coke.

When she came back with the ice and drinks, we headed out to the garden and then down a gravel path lined with the neatly spaced pines.

I stopped on the path. "This is so weird."

"What?"

"These trees."

"I think they're JNF—Jewish National Fund—trees. You know, planted by the State."

"But look." I pointed.

"What?"

"They're all the same."

"Yeah, so?"

"It's weird. It's not really a forest—too unnatural. There's no undergrowth."

"It's the Mediterranean, not like home."

"But they're all evenly spaced. It's like there was a clear-cut here and then someone said, 'Let's plant trees.'"

"Oh, I read about that." Aviva started walking again. "They've changed some of their policies since the fifties. I guess they didn't know much about diversity then, and some of the forests have burned down or have diseases. I think there's a plaque over there." Aviva pointed ahead.

We stopped by a simple stone monument.

"What does it say?"

Aviva paused to read the Hebrew. "It commemorates the soldiers who died while taking the hill in the 1948 War of Independence. There was probably a village here."

"What do you mean?"

"Probably some Arab village."

I turned to look at Aviva. "They planted trees over an Arab village?"

"Sure."

"Why would they do that?"

Aviva shrugged. "To make the land beautiful, I guess."

I stared at her. Then I rubbed my temples. Aviva seemed like a stranger. My head buzzed. I wanted to say, *This is not a forest.* Instead I said, "What happened to the people who used to live here?"

Aviva shrugged. "I dunno." She turned back to the memorial and sighed. "Sometimes it doesn't feel like enough, being here. I want to give more. These soldiers"—she pointed to the plaque—"died for Israel."

I gazed at her, then at the stupid dwarf trees. What if each tree represented a person who used to live here?

Aviva hugged her arms around her. "We should get going or we'll be late."

"Yeah, sure. Let's get out of here," I mumbled.

"What?"

"Nothing. Let's go."

Nausea billowed through me during prayers. The singing seemed perfunctory, even rushed. All through dinner, amid the chatter, the blessings, I felt my stomach churning. Where had the Arab people who used to live here gone? Were they killed or did they just move somewhere else? And why didn't Aviva know? She knew so much else about Judaism and Israel.

After the meal Aviva went to hear the guest speaker. I tried to participate in a discussion called *What Does God Want?* A group of girls sat in a conference room sipping tea in their white Shabbos blouses and skirts. I looked down at my own almost identical outfit and felt blood pound in my temples. I sat down with the other girls, but I missed the introduction because I could see the trees through the window. The moonlight made them look like a silent, deadly army. They looked bloodthirsty, their sameness a uniform. I tried to turn my attention to the discussion. A girl was speaking, gripping the armrests of her chair, her earnest New York accent grating. "So I was sobbing in my car and I just didn't know what to do. And so I started praying to God to help me, and just then, Sari came over and knocked on my window." She tipped her head to the girl sitting beside her. "Sari asked if I was okay, if she could help, and I just knew God had sent her." The two girls clasped hands.

We were supposed to work in small discussion groups. While the other girls were rearranging their chairs, I quietly left.

Up in my room I sat in the dark, just the Shabbos nightlight casting an eerie glow. I pulled an upright chair to the window and looked at the garden from between the ugly yellow curtains. A half-moon illuminated the garden, the trees casting long shadows. Voices echoed in the hallway, then all was quiet. I could hear the sound of my own breath.

For years every spring my Bubbie Bess had sent me a certificate saying she had planted a tree in Israel in my honor as part of a tree-planting holiday funded by the Jewish National Fund. The certificates had the words *A tree has been planted in honor of Mia Quinn by her Bubbie Bess* written in script beside a picture of two children in pointed pioneer hats planting a sapling. I kept the certificates in a box with other important papers. I'd even imagined a plaque with my name adorning a grove of trees. I thought Bess was planting fruit trees for children in my honor.

Once when I was down in Florida visiting Bess at her condo, I asked her about those tree certificates. We were alone by the pool, reclining on lawn chairs covered with monogrammed towels. Bess took off her glasses and let them dangle on their chain over the saggy bust of her pink muumuu. "I'll tell you, *mameleh,* why I send those trees to Israel. Because even if you don't know much about it, you're a Jew, and Israel is a safe place for you, if you ever need it. You'll always be okay in Toronto, but just as a backup, there's another place for you to go. And if you want to live there, they'll take you right away. They'll say, 'Mia Quinn, daughter of Sheila Katz, granddaughter of Bess and Abe Katz, we have you on our list. You are welcome to live here.'"

I didn't know much else about Israel until Aviva suggested I come to yeshiva with her. Before that, Israel was a foreign, shadowy topic on the nightly news.

Aviva's mom, Mrs. Blume, showed me slides from one of her trips to Israel. She sat me on her living-room couch one Saturday night and turned on a slide projector. A view of green hills and lakes hovered on the wall. She turned to me. "When I think of Israel," she began,

"I always think of the Jews who arrived there after World War Two: Holocaust survivors who lived through camps like Auschwitz or Bergen-Belsen. Those Jews survived the worst tragedy of the twentieth century. They'd been tortured and starved and were disease-ridden. Then they had a chance to start over again, and not in anti-Semitic Europe but in their own country, promised to them in the Torah. They were coming out of the slavery of Egypt, but instead of Pharaoh, it was Hitler. Instead of sheep to the slaughter, they became warriors in the land of milk and honey. Of course it wasn't like it is now; there were malaria swamps and the land had been left to fester under Ottoman rule. The Arabs had done nothing to develop the country."

Mrs. Blume gripped my shoulder. "I imagine those survivors getting off the ship and being handed guns to fight for something they really needed: a homeland." As Mrs. Blume spoke, she showed me slides of waterfalls in the north, temples in Jerusalem, southern deserts and the Tel Aviv coast.

I spent the next few months reading the novel *Exodus* and a book about the women of the Bible. Many nights when I closed my book I'd lie in bed, too charged up to sleep. I imagined people fleeing a land of snow and dirt, fleeing ravaging Cossacks and bloodthirsty Nazis, fleeing to freedom in a sun-drenched land ready to be planted, harvested and re-peopled. It made me think of my mother's favorite protest songs: Dylan doing "The Times They Are a-Changin'" and Pete Seeger singing "If I Had a Hammer." I imagined myself in Israel, walking in the desert, tracing the footpaths of my foremothers Sarah, Rachel, Rebecca and Leah. I'd visit the shops and streets where Holocaust victims became survivors, where the nearly dead became warriors. Like Hannah Senesh, who died trying to rescue Jews from the Nazis, or like the red-haired girl in *Exodus,* I'd be a religious warrior princess, studying Torah, traveling the land and celebrating Shabbos.

Now I stared up at the stippled ceiling of our bland room in a hotel in the middle of those weird trees. Mrs. Blume had never said anything about people already living here. I'd never really thought about Palestinians. They were men wrapped in scarves throwing rocks at Israeli soldiers on the news. I knew they committed terrorist acts, but I'd never thought about why they did them.

I tried to think of the shade the trees cast, the individual needles, the solid strength of each one growing out of that rocky soil, each tree representing a pioneer, a Jew who needed a homeland. But other people used to live here, had raised children and crops on this land. The trees seemed paltry, even miserable, in comparison. I mean, I loved trees, but not more than people.

I couldn't concentrate the next day during prayers. Through the windows I could see that creepy army of trees. I kept thinking, There are trees instead of people so Jews like me could come to Israel. I had to take a few deep breaths to calm the panic rising in my chest.

After lunch I went for a walk alone in the forest. It was very hot and the repetitive lines of trees made me feel dizzy. I'd never seen a forest without shade and fallen branches. It was like a tree museum or a tree farm. Worse, it felt dead, like a tree graveyard. "These people should stick to desert," I murmured. These people? What did that mean? I rushed back up the hill to the retreat center, trying to get out of the forest as fast as I could.

When the sun finally fell behind the hills and we'd sung the *havdalah* blessings marking the end of Shabbos, we boarded the bus back to the B'nos Sarah dorm. I couldn't wait to go.

Back in the dorm I lay on my bed in our darkened room with a damp washcloth over my face. My head ached from clenching my teeth. I could hear the voices of happy girls in the lounge. I wished they'd all go out and leave me alone. I hadn't slept well the night before.

Aviva knocked on our door and leaned her head in. "You okay?"

I lifted the washcloth and squinted at the light from the hall. "Headache."

"Will you be okay to play?"

"Play what?"

"Remember, the *kumzitz*?"

I groaned. "Oh right." I'd agreed to play guitar for a sing-along.

Aviva brought me some painkillers and sat on my bed while I got dressed. She had a tan from sitting out in the garden and was wearing a new pair of sandals.

I followed Aviva through the quiet hallways of the school. She poked my ribs. "What's with the serious look? It's Saturday night." She gave a little skip.

"I'm still thinking about the trees."

"What trees?"

"At the retreat center."

"What about them?" We went into the second-floor lounge, and Aviva flicked on the lights.

"Doesn't it bother you that the Jews took over land where other people were living?"

"No, it was our land." Aviva started moving chairs to form a circle.

"Yes, but other people lived here."

Chani and Rifka came in with some other girls, carrying bottles of juice, cups and bags of chips. Aviva waved at them and then turned back to me. "That's true, but they weren't supposed to."

"What are you guys talking about?" Chani asked.

"Oh, just Palestinians."

Chani nodded and joined the other girls in arranging the chairs.

Aviva turned back to me. "God promised the land to the Jews, not the others."

"So where were the Palestinians supposed to live?"

"There were no Palestinians before '48. They invented that identity. Before that they were just Arabs and they should have gone to Jordan or Lebanon to live in Arab countries." She smiled and walked away to get more chairs. "Hey, Mia, Ruthie brought the guitar."

I silently took the guitar and absently started tuning it. The other girls chattered and danced around the room. What was an invented identity? Israel was a young country. Wasn't their culture made up from scratch? What was all the tree planting about anyway? It was true there were lots of other Arab countries and only one Jewish country. Still, there had been people living in a village where now there were only trees. My head started to ache again.

More girls filed in, picked up song sheets and sat down. I strummed some bluegrass licks to warm up my fingers, and then I played "Amazing Grace," the first song I learned on banjo.

Aviva stared at me as if I'd become an alien, so I laid the guitar down on my lap and drummed my fingers on it until Aviva called the group to order.

She led the girls in singing "*Lo Yisa Goy El Goy Cherev.*" Nation shall not lift up sword against nation. The girls belted out the song, hands clapping and feet stamping.

I strummed along furiously, trying to keep up with their pace.

Then the girls sang a slower song about Jerusalem, *"Yerushalayim Shel Zahav."* Jerusalem of Gold. They draped their arms around each other's shoulders and swayed as they sang.

> *Oh, Jerusalem of gold,*
> *And of light and of bronze,*
> *I am the lute for all your songs.*

As their voices curled up toward the ceiling, my mind wandered back to what Aviva had said about the Palestinians. Did the rest of the girls think the same things? Chani and the others hadn't even been interested in the discussion.

I couldn't stand the way trees were being used. Trees were part of the natural world, like lakes and mountains. They were God's creation. They were supposed to just be. Sure, people chopped them down, like when Grandma Quinn's willow was razed, but how could they be used so violently?

When the *kumzitz* was over, Chani lingered behind. "Hey, Mia?"

"Yeah?"

"I bet you know how to play lots of other songs."

"Sure."

Chani lowered her voice. "Do you know how to play that Jaywalkers' song, the one that's always on the radio at home?" She sang the first line.

I hesitated. I thought of Don reading those terrible lyrics to us in our kitchen, and then I thought of us all up at the cottage. For a moment my mind wandered and I was under the birch trees at the shore. I shook my head. "Sorry, I don't know that one."

I went back up to my room and chose a postcard of a waving Israeli flag.

Dear Don,
Where you are, trees are part of nature. Here, they are acts of violence.

I didn't send it.

SIX

The next morning I found Michelle already reading the lesson in our Torah class. She hadn't come to the retreat because she'd wanted to spend Shabbos studying for her conversion. She looked more pale and drawn than usual.

Michelle looked up. "How was the retreat?"

I sat down. "Okay. Restful, sort of. It was in kind of a weird place."

"How so?"

"It was in this forest, but not a real forest, a planted one."

"Oh, I've been to one of those. It's amazing."

I tried not to frown. She looked so happy.

Michelle beamed. "I went on *Tu B'shvat*, the New Year of the Trees, and I got to plant my own tree."

Her face glowed with pleasure. "We went to this place—even movie stars plant trees there—and I had this little sapling and I put it in the ground with my own hands. Did you know there's a special prayer just for that? I felt just like a *kibbutznik* planting trees to drain the swamps."

Michelle looked so happy I didn't tell her about the village underneath the trees.

After classes I went to the Old City. I couldn't face the empty feeling of the *Kotel,* so I went to the Tower of David Museum, an enormous stone citadel near Jaffa Gate.

Icy air blasted me as I walked through displays depicting the history of Jerusalem: marauding Greeks, crusading Christians, invading Mameluks and, finally, the homecoming of the Jews. I chose a chair below an air-conditioning vent and let goose bumps form on my skin. I watched a film about Israeli independence twice in a row. The crowds cheered, waved flags and danced the *horah*. Behind me I could hear a Holocaust film from the previous display.

I yawned and checked my watch. The trees were plaguing my sleep. I dreamed of vines running rampant, strangling people while they ate their breakfasts, devouring them as they read the evening paper. When I tried to pray at school, I saw those trees between the words on the page. I squirmed in my chair. I could go back to the dorm and sweat in front of my fan or to school for a drop-in Hebrew session. Neither option appealed.

Heat smacked me in the chest as I left the air-conditioned exhibit hall. A sheen of sweat instantly broke out under the brim of my hat. I followed the labyrinthine paths of the citadel to a lookout tower. The Dome glimmered across the Old City's church spires, hydro wires, TV antennas and hot-water tanks. Down the street I could see a hostel with mattresses spread out on the roof. That must be where Andrew lived. He hadn't been on Ben Yehuda since the afternoon we went to the bar. Now there was just the traffic to listen to while waiting for the bus. Andrew would probably know about the trees. He would have some outside perspective. Yes, I could ask him.

I headed out of the museum and marched in the direction of the hostel. Twice I walked down dead-end streets, until I asked for directions.

In the lobby of the hostel, a large man with an untucked shirt talked on the phone behind a counter. A young woman in a gauzy sundress and several toe rings sat on a couch painting her toenails. A henna tattoo snaked around her biceps. She made me think of the bars I used to play at in Toronto.

I paused to study a bulletin board. Bongo drums and a Serratus backpack were for sale. Peace Now was looking for volunteers to rebuild houses. Three American women wanted a non-smoking roommate. All were welcome to attend a Jewish meditation course in Sefat. Flyers advertised car rentals, a Chinese buffet and tours to the Golan, the Galilee and the Negev.

Faintly, I could hear people singing and playing guitars.

"Where's the music coming from?" I asked the man behind the counter.

He pointed toward a tiled staircase. "The roof."

The music, U2's "One," grew louder as I climbed up six flights. Rows of drying laundry lined one side of the roof. On the other side loomed the Dome of the Rock and the Citadel, with the Mount of Olives behind. A group of travelers sat in the shade of an outstretched tarp on an assortment of rickety stools, rough benches and crates. Two blond guys in jean cutoffs and ball-caps led the song on guitars, toes tapping in their sport sandals. From the top of the staircase I could see Andrew strumming along, his back to me. The round chords of the song reverberated across the roof. I started singing along.

I paused at the edge of the circle and dug my nails into my wrists to fight the urge to push up the sleeves of my plain T-shirt. I imagined the travelers thinking, What the hell is someone dressed like that doing here?

I wouldn't stay for the music. I'd just ask Andrew about the trees; then I'd be off. I hovered behind him until the song finished. When he saw me, one light brown eyebrow slid toward his hairline. "Hey, sandwich girl, good to see you. Have a seat."

"I can't stay."

"You playing hooky again?"

I laughed and shook my head.

"Not for one song?"

"Well..."

The musicians started playing "I Still Haven't Found What I'm Looking For."

"Um...okay." I started singing along again.

Secular music wasn't really what my life was about now, but it was only for a few minutes. I found a chair among the lines of drying laundry, and Andrew moved over to let me in. A blond woman with a violin offered me a beer. I hesitated and then accepted. The icy bitterness instantly made me feel cooler. A joint made its way around the circle. I held it a moment, letting the sweet smell tickle my nostrils, then passed it along without inhaling. It reminded me of listening to Led Zeppelin with Matt.

The U2 song ended and someone struck up "Country Roads." My hands ached to play.

"You want?" Andrew held out his guitar.

I shook my head.

"Here, c'mon. You look like you know this one."

I hesitated and then reached for the guitar. "Like the back of my hand."

I wanted to take off my hat and shake my sweaty hair out of my tight braids. I wiped my forehead with the back of my hand instead. I played G, E minor, D, my voice quietly harmonizing with the others.

"Yeah," one of the blond guys called out.

"Sounds good," another said.

I relaxed into the familiar chords and let my head tip back, my eyes close. My mom's friend Deirdre used to play the song at Sheila's potluck guitar nights. I'd fall asleep to the music, the smell of chili lingering in the air.

The song ended and the blond guys launched into a Beatles' *Abbey Road* medley. I held the guitar out to Andrew, but he folded his arms across his chest. "I'm sure you know this too."

I strummed along. "Actually, I came to ask you something."

"What's up?" Andrew leaned back in his chair.

Around me the others sang, "*You never give me your money.*" I stopped playing the guitar and hugged it to my chest. I didn't know where to start. "It's about the trees here. I thought maybe you would know something about them. I don't know very much about politics. Well, nothing at all." I paused and tried to think of what to say next. Andrew sat, eyes wide, listening intently, ignoring the others around us. I felt my cheeks redden. "I'm going to start all over again."

"Take your time."

The travelers sang, *"And in the middle of negotiation, you break down."* The guitar felt good in my hands, like I was sitting in an old familiar position.

I took a deep breath. "I was at this retreat this weekend, near Jerusalem, and there was this forest... well, it wasn't really a forest, more like a park. Planted trees, one of those JNF forests—that means Jewish National Fund. I don't know if you know about them. And then, all of a sudden it dawned on me—you'll think this is really stupid—but there was this plaque that talked about the soldiers who died taking over the area. I guess I thought Israel was an empty country or that all the Arabs took off when the Jews arrived. I don't know if I read that or—or if I just thought that."

"I think half the country is built over former Arab villages."

"Doesn't that bother you?" I felt my forehead wrinkle. "I know there was a war and all, but I didn't realize they did that with trees—planted over villages."

Andrew narrowed his eyes. "You win the war, you keep the land."

"I know. I just...well, maybe I didn't know."

"The government is still taking over land." His face lost its usual teasing grin.

"Really?"

"Sure. There's this girl here, Sonia, who works for some peace organization. She was saying they force Palestinians to sell their land so they can build more Jewish housing."

"That's terrible."

Andrew shrugged. "They don't recognize the Palestinians as citizens."

I cracked my knuckles in my lap. "It seems so twisted to use trees to claim the land. I mean, I love trees."

Andrew nodded.

"My grandmother used to send money to plant those JNF trees."

"Uh-huh."

I sighed and hugged my arms around me. "I was hoping you'd say something reassuring."

"Like?"

"I don't know. That it's for a greater cause. My room-mate says it was our land to start with."

Andrew rested one foot on his other knee. "And what do you think of that?"

"I'm not sure what to think. I always thought being Jewish meant being moral and taking the higher ground."

"Seems to me the Jews are always killing for their land."

My face grew hot. "That's because the Jews are always under attack. Someone is always trying to take away our land. And what about the Holocaust? Where were the Jews supposed to go after that?"

Andrew shrugged. "Displacing other people only makes more problems. We should get Sonia over here. Hey, Sonia."

85

A thin girl wearing a bandanna over short dark hair looked at us across the circle. She had a nose ring and a tattoo of the sun on her exposed shoulder. Andrew motioned her over. "Mia and I were just talking politics, and I was telling her that you were our local expert."

Sonia grinned and shook her head. "What do you want to know?"

"We were discussing what happened to the Palestinians after '48. They all moved away, right?" He winked at me.

Sonia gripped her bony hands together. "Some people left, but others had to flee, and others were killed."

I leaned forward. "Why didn't they go to Arab countries?"

"They weren't wanted there and they still aren't. This is their homeland."

"So that's why there are terrorists?"

Sonia shook her head. "If you lost your homeland, wouldn't you fight for it? Jews created Israel through acts of terrorism against the British. Freedom fighter, terrorist—it all depends on your point of view."

Andrew said, "Most Palestinians just want clean water and good schools—basic human rights."

I nodded, trying to absorb everything. Jews had been terrorists too? Sonia and Andrew talked about the Palestinian leaders and whether they really wanted peace, and if negotiations with the Israeli government would ever proceed. Sonia said something about the UN being imperialistic, and I tried to remember what Aviva said about the UN's two-state solution. The guitarists played Elton John's "Rocket Man."

Sonia stood up. "I'm sorry but I have to get going. It was nice meeting you, Mia. Keep asking questions. I can recommend some books if you like."

I nodded. "Sure, thanks." I slouched back in my chair. "I don't understand politics at all."

Andrew smiled. "I don't get most of it either, but I do know one thing: there's a power imbalance. And it's not fair."

I sighed. "Power imbalance?" This was far more complicated than trees planted over a village.

"Israel is a first-world country with huge American financial backing. The Palestinians are a poor native people who have been uprooted." I must have given him a quizzical look. He sighed. "Have you ever walked the ramparts, the wall around the Old City?"

"Um, no. I've been wanting to go, but I didn't want to go alone."

"Your seminary buddies too busy?"

"Um, I guess so."

"Meet me at Jaffa Gate tomorrow after your classes. I'll take you on a tour."

I felt my cheeks flush. "That would be great," I whispered.

Andrew nodded. "Just one thing."

"What's that?"

"I wanna hear you play that song of your dad's, the one you were telling me about. The one about the trees."

"Oh, well, sure." I stood up. "Okay, bye then." I started backing away.

"So what time are you done?"

I stumbled over a crate and bent to rub my calf. "Um, two. If that's okay."

"See you at two." Andrew gave me another one of his sexy grins, and I felt heat flood my face again, like the Jerusalem sun blazing through me.

I could hear the chords to Don's tree song in my head as I waited at the bus stop. Don had played the song for me the previous summer at his cottage, just before we went home. We were up on the saggy porch watching the squirrels run along the railing to take the nuts Sheila had put out.

> You said you could always come home,
> But it'd never be the same.
> Oh, Momma, I'm getting old as you,
> But I fear I'll never be as wise.

I lay stretched out in a hammock on the rickety screened-in porch. Don's other songs revealed glimpses of the mystery of his life: songs of driving, of working on

a beet farm, of hiding out in a barn in Peterborough, of
a field of wild flowers. But this song, I knew it exactly.
I'd been in love with Grandma Quinn's willow too.

Call off the bulldozers,
Call off our western ways.
This progress, I'll have none of it,
'Cause I lost my weeping willow where I used to sit.

The summer I was twelve, Don took me on a car
trip to West Virginia to visit his mother, my Grandma
Quinn. I had never been away with just Don, and I was
thrilled to spend time with him. The rare times Don
stayed at our house, he barely hung out with us. He
would lie on the couch, his legs hanging off the edge of
the armrest, listening to old blues singers who sounded
like they carried heavy burdens. He said he needed still-
ness to chase away the rumble of the car after being on
tour so long. Sometimes he'd take me with him on his
walks along the Beaches' boardwalk. I'd dance around
him doing cartwheels, talking nonstop, not expecting
answers. Anything Don said was like a little nugget of
gold to keep, no matter how banal. I kept his comments
in my head the way other girls kept trinkets in a jewelry
box: study hard at school, try to see all points of view,
take a deep breath every now and then.

I had spent the first part of that summer at a socialist
camp singing "We Shall Overcome" and learning about

Mother Jones. Three weeks of bunk beds, communal showers, sweating around a campfire, chanting "white rabbit, white rabbit" whenever the smoke blew my way. Three weeks of splashing dock noise, rec-hall rumble, dinner-hall chanting and late-night giggles.

All the way to West Virginia, Don sat silent on the sticky bench seat of his Buick. Every few hours he'd squint his green eyes and reach for the small spiral notebook he kept tucked in the sun visor. He'd scribble a few lines in his bird-claw scrawl, the notebook balanced delicately on the steering wheel.

"So"—I rested my feet on the dash—"this is what you do."

Don stroked his beard. I could see the dimple in his chin through the gray. "Yes. I drive and I think. Then I stop and I play songs."

"What do you think about?"

Don paused so long I thought he wouldn't answer. Then he said, "I think about my street, and the tree in Grandma Quinn's yard—it's an old weeping willow. I think about the poems she read to us before we went to sleep. We were very poor. I don't remember wanting a lot, other than a bicycle."

"And?"

Another long pause. "Sometimes I think about important questions."

"Like?"

"I think, where have I been and where am I going? Who am I? If you've got those figured out, life's easy."

I scrunched up my face, peering at him. Those were the important questions? A cinch! I was Mia Quinn, daughter of Don Quinn and Sheila Katz. Where had I been? I'd been to Bowmore Senior Public School. Next I was off to Monarch Park Collegiate. Easy.

On the second day, Don sat me in the backseat and gave me his guitar. "We'll pretend we're on tour and you're in the band. When we get to Arlington, you'll play for your gran."

I practiced "Country Roads" and Neil Young's "Harvest Moon." Over and over I strummed the chorus of the Indigo Girls' "Closer to Fine."

When we arrived, Grandma Quinn was in her back garden sitting in a lawn chair among hollyhocks and sunflowers. She wore a mauve floral-print house-dress and stout beige leather shoes. Her long white hair was spread out over the back of her chair. I stared at the blue tinge radiating down the strands like tie-dye. "I thought I'd best give it a wash before you came," Grandma Quinn said, coiling her hair into a neat bun at the nape of her neck. She turned to me. "I like blue. It's my favorite color."

Grandma Quinn's narrow clapboard house seemed to sway when anyone climbed the stairs. Crocheted doilies covered each chair and end table in the tidy living room. A photograph from the early sixties of Don and his brothers and sisters—Ted, Bill, Therese and Iris—rested on top of the television. The carpet was worn and the crockery old, but the house was spotless. "I have a girl who comes and cleans once a week," Grandma Quinn explained. "I can't see the dirt anymore. What a blessing." I slept upstairs in a narrow bed with a faded patchwork quilt. A large wooden crucifix hung on the wall above my head.

In the morning Don busied himself fixing the back gate, nailing down loose boards in the porch, and tidying the basement. I sat on the stone patio and played the guitar for Grandma Quinn while she weeded her garden.

"Very nice," she said. "You must have a good teacher."

"My dad teaches me, when he's around."

"Oh." Grandma Quinn smiled.

I nodded. "So, who helps you with the garden?"

"Ah, that I can see. I grow tall plants now. I like to sit and have them tower over me."

Grandma Quinn went back to weeding. Beyond the porch and the flower beds, a giant weeping willow dominated the lawn. The branches cascaded like waterfalls, trailing almost to the grass. What made a tree's branches reach toward the ground instead of the sky? I wanted to sit underneath it and see what it would be like to be surrounded by all that green, but it seemed a babyish thing to do.

In the afternoon Don's sister Therese came by with butter tarts. She had the same narrow face, widow's peak, auburn hair and pale green-gray eyes as Don and me. I couldn't stop staring at her. I thought, That's how I'll look when I'm older.

Don, Therese and Grandma Quinn talked about people I didn't know. I strummed the guitar a few minutes and walked the little path among the flowers. I stood, face upturned, looking at the willow. It was a giant shaggy monster. No, it was a million dancers' hands. I parted the leaves and entered the green and gold cave. The leaves shimmered and cast dappled shade over the grass. I sat with my back against the trunk and listened. Don's voice melded with the sound of the breeze blowing the rustling leaves. I watched an ant crawl through the grass, the strands an obstacle course. I let my eyes close. I was strangely relaxed, almost sleepy.

For dinner we ate cold cuts and coleslaw and drank icy lemonade. As the light faded, Don played "Old Gray Mare" and "Hesitation Blues" on a banjo Therese had brought over. He and Therese sang "Not A-Gonna Lay My Religion Down," stomping out the beat with their feet.

I'd heard this music before on my dad's records, but I'd never heard it played live. I came out from under the tree to listen.

"I didn't know you knew how to play those songs."

Don shrugged.

"We used to sing those as kids," Therese explained. "Our dad taught us. We would stand at the foot of the willow tree as if it were a stage, tie back the branches like curtains and put on a show for Ma and my dad before he died. We'd be the Warbling Quinn Sisters and Banjo Ted, or the Billy-Hilly Brothers with Chanteuse Therese. The boys would play garbage cans, plastic buckets and Mama Quinn's pots. Ba-bah-*bahm*! Ba-bah-*bahm*! Until our oldest brother, Bill, brought home a banjo, that is. I never saw your dad want anything so bad."

"Can you teach me to play that?" I asked Don.

"Banjo?"

"Yes."

Therese laughed. "Look at her. She's hooked."

Don handed me the banjo, and I took it back to the base of the tree and started plucking the strings.

Before we left the next day to drive back to Toronto, Don stopped at a pawn shop and bought me a five-string bluegrass banjo. I sat in the backseat all the way home, and Don taught me to play "Amazing Grace."

I saw my bus coming slowly down the street, starting and stopping in the traffic. I edged forward into the crowd, hoping to get a seat. My hands pressed the chords to Don's tree song against my legs.

Trees, the Earth's angels, without you we will fade.
You are our mothers and our fathers;
We have sold you for an easy buck,
Hoping to endure by luck.

I understood this song because I had fallen in love with Grandma Quinn's willow. And now it was gone, along with her house and garden. It wasn't the same to sit under a birch or poplar or even a maple.

I boarded the bus back to B'nos Sarah. I could easily remember the chords to Don's song, if I had a guitar. Shit, women weren't supposed to play for men. Well, stupid, if you're not supposed to play music for guys, you're not supposed to go running around historic sites with them either. Oh please, he was just like a tour guide or a friend. Crap. I wasn't supposed to have male friends or even be alone with guys. Well, we wouldn't be alone, we were meeting in a public place, so it would be fine. Right? Right. I clenched my boring skirt in my fists.

⟪

Andrew was waiting for me at Jaffa Gate the next afternoon. He was wearing shorts, another shabby T-shirt, this one with the name of a band I didn't know, and sandals. I averted my eyes from his tanned legs.

"So, ready to explore?"

"Yes, let's." I clasped my hands behind me and followed Andrew up a steep flight of stairs. "Have you walked here before?"

"Oh yeah."

"Do you really think it's not safe to go alone?"

"Maybe for a girl. Pickpockets might be the worst problem."

The path between the two walls was too narrow to walk side by side. I tried to ignore Andrew's sweaty back by looking out over the rooftop solar tanks.

We stopped at Damascus Gate to peer down at the vendors below. People swarmed in and out of the gate. Beyond the Old City, traffic seethed in the heat. I watched baby chicks scramble over each other in a box. Andrew waited patiently, lounging in the shade. Behind us, the Dome gleamed close by. I pointed to it. "I never knew a building could be so amazing. Have you been?"

"Yes." Andrew leaned against the rampart wall. His eyes were hidden behind his sunglasses; it made him seem distant, a stranger.

"How was it?"

"Interesting. You should go."

I scrunched up my face. "I wanted to, but then I found out it's on top of the holiest place in Judaism. Jews aren't supposed to walk there." I thought he'd roll his eyes or snicker, but he just nodded.

"I can't believe the history you can see from here. Everything from the Mameluks to the Ottomans and"— I turned and swept my arm across modern Jerusalem— "all of the present."

"Everything?" Andrew crossed his arms against his chest.

"Huh?"

"I said 'everything?'"

"Well, no, of course not, but you know what I mean—there's a huge range of history here."

"I suppose."

"What are you getting at?"

"Excavation and building are always political."

"Sure, but there's a quarter for everyone here. Christians here, Muslims over there."

"Yeah, but this area is like layers of a cake. You want British remains, dig this deep." He held his thumb and forefinger a few inches apart. "You want Muslim ruins, then dig this deep." Fingers farther apart. "It's a Jewish country and so the government lets archaeologists dig through all those layers to find what they want."

"Oh, right." I knew that. Didn't I? Maybe I just hadn't thought of it that way.

"Have you walked in the Muslim section of the city?" he asked.

"Just a little." I'd darted through the Arab market once.

"It's not as fancy as the Jewish section, huh?"

I nodded my head. "I guess not."

We continued walking around the Old City. The ramparts were less interesting than I imagined. Mostly I saw hot-water tanks. The view was better from Andrew's hostel.

When we got back to Jaffa Gate, I followed Andrew down the narrow, dim staircase to the street. Halfway down, a group of kids came rushing and yelling up the stairs, and Andrew stopped abruptly. I crashed into his hot back, burying my nose in the skin of his neck. I found myself closing my eyes and inhaling deeply, unconsciously. He smelled musky, not cologne-scented, but with a hint of soap and the tanginess of sweat. I could feel the heat of him. For a moment I was suspended, bodiless, just taking in his scent. I wanted to stay there forever, but then the kids were gone and their teacher was apologizing in English and Hebrew as she came up the stairs, her tiny frame dwarfed by an enormous backpack.

Down on the street the sun dazzled my eyes. I wanted to lean in and breathe Andrew's sweet smell again. A dribble of sweat arced down my cheek. My pulse pounded. I wanted to say, I smelled you and you're not who I thought you were.

"I have to get going." I backed away from him.

"Come back to the hostel for a drink first."

"Not today." I resisted the urge to flee.

"Are you feeling okay?"

"Yes, fine, just a little too hot. Maybe sunstroke. Have to go now."

"Wait, I'm playing at an open-mic night at a bar in Tel Aviv. You should come." He pulled a flyer out of his pocket.

"Oh, well. Maybe." I took the paper from him and continued to back away.

"I still want to hear that song you were telling me about."

"Right. Some other time." I walked away as quickly as I could without breaking into a run.

When I got home I stripped off my clothes and got in the shower, letting the cold water pound over me until my teeth chattered and my head filled with a blinding blue light. I poured myself a large glass of juice, dished up a bowl of olives and a stinky piece of cheese and lay on my bed. I took a big slug of juice and ate three olives.

He smelled like…like something I thought maybe I'd been looking for, like…I ground my fists into my eyes until I saw stars.

Think, think about something else. I grabbed my prayer book off the desk and opened it randomly. I stood in my room, my face buried in the gluey-smelling pages and recited the ancient words until they obliterated any memory of Andrew's sweet smell.

SEVEN

"Mia, you're doing it again."

"What?"

"The finger tapping." Aviva and I were lying in bed trying to sleep. I could see her scowling at me in the dim light.

"Oh, sorry." I crossed my arms over my chest and tucked my hands into my armpits. I'd gone Israeli dancing with Chani and her friends, but I couldn't concentrate on the steps. My head had filled with thoughts of Andrew. I'd close my eyes and try to remember the feeling of my nose brushing against his neck. It was like falling or flying. It was better than being high, or sensing God, or singing with a group of people. It was intoxicating.

I sighed and Aviva rolled over noisily. I was supposed to come to yeshiva, deepen my understanding of Judaism and then meet some nice Jewish boy, get married and have kids. We'd celebrate the holidays and live a nice secure life. And here I was, mooning over a non-Jewish guy, a guitar player.

I decided to get out of bed. Aviva moaned when she heard my mattress creak. "Now what?"

"I think I'll sit up in the lounge for a while. I don't want to keep you awake."

Aviva groaned. "Fine."

The artificial glare of the lights in the lounge made me cringe so I headed up to the roof deck. I sat in a chair and looked out at the city's lights and water towers.

I just wouldn't see Andrew again—no problem. Then I thought about the handbill I'd shoved in my backpack. He was playing in a bar in Tel Aviv. I imagined him up on a stage, somewhere very French, with little candles on checkered tablecloths and lots of red wine, singing a song for me. Then he'd come over and kiss me and invite me to sing a duet. First we'd do "I Can't Help Falling in Love With You," and after the audience went nuts we'd do "Crazy."

Of course I wouldn't go. I'd try Israeli dancing with Chani and her friends again or stay home with Aviva and give her a guitar lesson.

After a while I got thirsty and bored and went back down to the hot little box of our room and lay in my narrow bed. Aviva breathed deeply from her side of the room. I felt like lobbing a spitball to see if she'd wake up.

I'd never been in love before. In my observation, being in love only led to heartbreak and disappointment. My friend Kayla was always yearning for some guy or devastated by a betrayal. She fell in love with our chemistry teacher (who turned her down); then it was some college guy. She went out with Dave Ng until he dumped her for Lisa Camble. Who wanted all that gut-churning emotional trauma? But now, here I was, mooning over Andrew.

I finally fell asleep, dreaming of his wrists and the way he held his guitar, his narrow hips, his sweet, sweet smell.

The next morning I joined Chani and her friends Sarah and Rifka on the couch in the B'nos Sarah lounge before class.

Chani sat on the armrest, radiating enthusiasm. "He's really cute and he's from the same part of New Jersey as me, and next year he'll be at Columbia." The other girls listened attentively. I pretended to be excited for her too.

One of the girls turned to Chani and sang out, "*Kol chatan v'kol kallah.*"

"What's that mean?" I asked.

"It's the song she's hoping to hear after her next date with Yosef!" Sarah said.

"What?"

Chani spoke over the singing girls. "They're just being silly. It's the song you sing when someone gets engaged or married." I nodded and tried to smile.

Why the hell would anyone want to get married so young? Okay, Chani was older than me, but she was still only twenty. There were so many things I wanted to do first, like scuba dive, see Paris and go to university. I hadn't been to Nashville yet or learned to speak Italian. Maybe I'd had enough sex in high school to get some of the boy-craziness out of my system. I shook my head. Maybe everyone here was just really eager to get laid. That had to be it.

I'd learned about Orthodox marriages when I first started going to Aviva's parents' house for dinner. I'd go to the Blumes' early and help Aviva chop vegetables or set the table. One night as were setting the table I got up the courage to ask Aviva if she knew any boys.

Aviva cocked her head to the side. "My brothers and cousins and nephews. Sometimes I talk to my neighbor's son, Jacob. I've known him all my life."

"But you don't date or anything, right?"

"No. Have you dated anyone?" Aviva looked curious.

A vision of having sex with Matt flashed through my head. We'd never really dated; no one I knew did. At school people hooked up at parties. "Neh, not really."

Aviva lowered her voice. "Have you ever kissed a boy?"

I cracked a toe on the linoleum floor. "Yeah."

Aviva giggled. "Have you ever—"

"So, I was wondering about how you get married," I said quickly. "I don't understand why you can't even hold hands with a guy."

Aviva handed me wineglasses from the dining room buffet. "If you start to feel, you know, romantic about someone, it's hard to make an objective decision about whether they're the best person for you. You know, if you have the same life goals and plans."

"Wow." I wasn't sure what else to say. Aviva giggled and started laying out cutlery. I thought about Matt. Did we have any similar life goals? Only to get high, make music and have sex. I tried imagining my parents on a date in the early seventies, discussing life plans. Sheila would have said she wanted to have kids, and Don would have run the other way. I laid a fork on top of a blue folded napkin. Maybe it wasn't such a bad idea, getting to know someone first. "What if you don't know what your plans or goals are?"

"Your teachers or parents wouldn't try and set you up if they thought you weren't ready."

I nodded again. "But what about being in love?"

"My sister Malka says she fell in love with her husband, Tsvi, on their very first date. Isn't that sweet?"

I nodded. "Sounds great."

I wasn't totally convinced, but I could see the logic. I'd slept with Matt because I thought he really liked me, and then I'd been disappointed when he ditched me. If you were Orthodox and you got set up with someone who had the same goals as you, then you wouldn't be let down. Aviva made the Orthodox way of getting married sound almost sexy. I guess you'd be really hot for some action if you had to wait until you married. I thought, Hell, if I could be a reborn Jew, maybe I could be a reborn virgin too.

When I got to my Torah class, Michelle wasn't there. Her notebook with the cats on the cover lay on the table where we usually studied. On the inside cover, Michelle had taped a photograph of a thin, blond woman with waist-length feathery hair, wearing a plaid work shirt. I wondered if it was her mom. In the top corner was Michelle's Jerusalem address and phone number.

I tried to study alone but I found myself doodling in my notebook. I designed a blouse with a mandarin collar and long narrow sleeves. I shaded side panels in a slightly darker color, so you'd look slimmer. What about a calf-length skirt with an angled hemline? Would that work? I added a scandalously tall pair of boots. I sighed and put down the pen. I had bought several boring skirts and tops from one of the stores the girls here all talked about. Every morning I shuddered a little as I put on my beige skirt and pastel T-shirt.

My fingers kept returning to my pocket, and the dog-eared handbill for Andrew's concert. He was playing tonight. I looked around the room at the other girls, all engaged in discussions. They searched through the texts, took notes and consulted the Torah teacher. They all seemed so content with their learning, dancing and volunteer work. It was like they'd all drunk a magic happiness potion. The newly religious girls almost glowed.

After my first class I gave up trying to study and went back to the empty dorm, taking Michelle's notebook with me. I couldn't face a whole morning trying to read Hebrew alone. I lay on the couch in the common room and watched reruns of *Beverly Hills 90210*. When I got bored, I dialed Michelle's number. I got no answer, so I went for a run.

I'd become bored with my relentlessly steep route up Mount Scopus, so I decided to run out another way, past the edge of the city. I headed out on a steadily inclined path, and soon I was past the city streets. One side of the road was mountainside, the other a drop-off to the desert. The heat was oppressive—too hot for running. Still, I ran a little faster, excited by the landscape, my pulse escalating. I tried to ignore the road, keeping my vision on the view of the hills, until I was just a body moving through space. My breathing settled into a steady rhythm. Blood pulsed in my ears. I was breathing hard as I surged uphill. The way home would be easy. I could feel sweat behind my knees and trickling down my chest.

The road curved and became narrower. I could only see the immediate asphalt in front of me, the panorama of sand and hills on my right. Maybe I'd end up in an Arab community. A little thrill of nerves and anticipation made me run faster. Then, around the curve, I saw familiar four-story Jerusalem stone apartment blocks, the same kind of park, bank and grocery store as my own neighborhood. I was half relieved, half disappointed.

I ran up the main street. Two small girls stared at me as I went by in my jogging pants and baggy T-shirt. They wore long dresses and heavy tights. Farther ahead a group of boys with curly sidelocks twirled into ringlets stared at me. My head swiveled to gawk at small boys with curlers attached to the sides of their heads. Up by the market I passed women in wigs wearing long-sleeved dresses, and men in dark suits and fur hats. They stared at my running clothes. I turned abruptly and ran back the way I'd come. I'd entered a *haredi*, an ultra-Orthodox community.

On the way out a teenage boy hissed something in Hebrew at me. I guessed it meant "whore." I started running faster. Fuck you, I felt like yelling back. I ended up here by mistake. Who was he to say what was modest and what wasn't? He made me feel cheap, ugly.

That was it. I had to get out of Jerusalem. Tel Aviv was less than an hour away by bus. It would be just the thing: a little salt air, a little secular culture, an afternoon adventure. Perhaps with Michelle. The date of Andrew's gig was embossed in my thoughts.

Back at the dorm I stood in the communal shower stall with its peeling walls and let the cool water wash away the sweat and tired ache of heat in my bones. Then I dressed and packed a change of clothes along with my water bottle, guidebook and Michelle's notebook. Before I left I wrote a quick note for Aviva. *Staying late at volunteering and then meeting friends for dinner.*

Michelle rented a room in an apartment block near the yeshiva. Children's voices ricocheted up and down the shabby hallways of her building.

A woman in a head covering with two little children holding on to her skirt let me into a crowded apartment. "Her room is down the hall." She pointed and I skirted past a baby bathtub and stacks of plastic storage tubs.

Michelle sat at a small table reading a book, her head in her hands. The room was barren except for a bed with a faded cover and a dresser with a toiletries case on it. A hook on the wall held clothes on hangers. Michelle's shoes were neatly lined up in the corner of the room.

"Oh, hi." She looked surprised to see me. We'd never talked about where she lived.

"You left your book. I thought I'd bring it by."

"Thanks." She rubbed her face sleepily.

"Are you feeling okay?"

"Just a little anxious." She chewed on her thumbnail. "How did you know where to find me?"

"Your address was on the inside cover of your book."

"Oh, right."

"So, this is where you live." I hovered by the door.

"Yup."

"It's very...bare."

"I don't spend much time here."

"I missed you today."

Michelle nodded. "My conversion exam is really soon."

I nodded. "Oh. I'm thinking it's really, really hot in here and I'm going to Tel Aviv. I think you should come with me."

"I have to study."

"You need an afternoon off."

"That's what Shabbos is for."

"Right. And sometimes you need to rock out. We're going to the beach."

"My exam is in less than two weeks."

"You can study later. Or I'll quiz you on the bus. I need to get out of this city. Jerusalem's feeling really claustrophobic right now, and I need some sinners to make me look good. I hear Tel Aviv's just the thing."

Michelle hesitated.

"There'll be fresh sea breezes."

"Let me get my sunglasses."

When Michelle reached for her notebook to add to her backpack, I took it from her and chucked it on the bed. "Enough. Just bring a towel."

We took a city bus to the main bus terminal and then another bus to Tel Aviv. As the bus descended the steep, rocky hills of Jerusalem, we drove through more planted JNF trees. I shuddered and tried not to think about them. Then the road entered a lush plain. I squinted out the window as the sun shone through sprinklers irrigating crops. When I pointed them out to Michelle, she said, "Oranges. You should have been here in the spring. When I got off the plane, all I could smell was orange blossoms. It was amazing."

Less than an hour later we entered the sprawling outskirts of Tel Aviv. It looked like any other big city: traffic, shops, people walking with children.

From the Tel Aviv bus station we took a local bus down to the beach. The streets were wider than in Jerusalem, and the buildings seemed haphazard, almost slapdash, compared to Jerusalem's stone buildings.

Michelle flapped her shirt. "It's very humid."

"Isn't it great? My skin is absolutely drinking in the moisture."

We made our way down to the water and joined the parade of people strolling along the boardwalk. Gentle waves rolled over families splashing on the beach.

"Look how happy people are here. It's like a champagne cork got released."

"I haven't seen so much flesh in ages." Michelle stared at the swimmers.

"Don't you feel it? People are relaxed." We strolled along the promenade, passing couples arm in arm, families with children running about. Hair blew in the breeze over exposed shoulders. There were women with bare midriffs, shirtless men, young girls clad only in bikinis.

"You don't like Jerusalem?" Michelle's face had lost its hard lines, its furrowed brow. She looked pretty, wisps of blond hair blowing around her face.

"Of course I do. It's just good to get out. See the sea, feel the breeze, have a change in scenery. Sometimes I feel Jerusalem has too much emotion, too much religious expectation."

We pulled off our sandals and walked down to the water. Waves swirled around our ankles. My feet sank into the sand, my toes making shallow impressions.

"I'm going in. You coming?"

"What'll you wear after?"

"We'll just dry in the breeze."

"Well, okay."

We laid our backpacks on the shore where we could see them and walked into the waves. I let the water close over my head. When I surfaced I looked over at Michelle. "You look relaxed," I said.

"I'll feel even better once I pass my conversion."

"That'll be good."

"Yeah, I won't have to pretend anymore."

"Whaddya mean?" We bobbed in the waves.

"I'll have a Jewish name, and I'll be able to go on dates."

I nodded. "How does your family feel about your conversion?"

"I'm not in contact with them. My mom's dead."

"Oh, I'm sorry, I didn't know…" I thought about the picture of the woman on the inside cover of Michelle's notebook.

Michelle waved her hand. "It's been a year now. She wasn't well, you know, in her mind. It's better this way."

"What about the rest of your family?"

"I don't have a dad. My grandmother is in a rest home. My older sister lives in a trailer park with her kids in Kansas. We don't speak. Do you want me to go on?"

"Wow. No, that's okay." I felt a heaviness settle over me.

"I feel like I'm getting a new family though." Michelle brightened. "You and the other girls. It's all new and good." She smiled.

"That's great."

When we got out of the water, we walked all the way down to the end of the beach and back to dry off our clothes. The wind whipping our skirts and hair felt so good I practically danced along the shore.

Michelle turned to me. "Thanks for bringing me here."

"Like I said, sometimes you need a break." I twirled around. "And this is just the beginning. After this we're going to hear some music."

"You're kidding, right?"

"Where else do you have to be?"

"At home, studying."

"Right, just that crazy little room with your books."

"I don't do secular music anymore."

"Oh, c'mon. It'll be fun."

"No." Michelle crossed her arms over her chest. "Secular music was part of my old life."

"What, you want to be like the others, engaged at twenty?"

Michelle looked dreamy. "If it was the right guy. Besides, I'm already twenty-three."

"C'mon. Don't you think those girls, like Chani, going on *shidduch* dates, should live a little first, get some life experience?"

"I wouldn't want to go through all that again."

"All what?"

"You know." Michelle hesitated. "The drinking, the sleeping with people you don't care about."

"Don't you feel you had to go through all that to get here?"

"No. Absolutely not." Michelle pushed loose strands of her hair back into her ponytail.

"What if you'd never heard the Dead?"

Michelle waved a hand in the air. "What a waste of time. I could have been learning and celebrating *Hashem*. I was heading somewhere bad." Her face clouded. "But I'm going to be okay now."

"Yeah, I'm sure you are." We were back at the bus stop. "So, I guess I'll see you tomorrow."

"You're really not coming back?"

"I think I'll hang out a while longer. You can find your way, right?"

"Well, sure, but..." Michelle frowned.

I gave a little wave. "Not to worry."

I waited until Michelle's bus came. As soon as she was out of sight, I forgot about her. I was alone in Tel Aviv. I felt so normal, like any girl in a big city with plans for the night. I went into a hotel bathroom to change my clothes and wash some of the salt off my hands and face. I tried to comb out my hair but it was so tangled and frizzy from the salt and humidity, I rebraided it and put my hat back on.

The intensity of the sun was diminishing and the city had a post-workday feel. I glanced at the address on the flyer Andrew had given me and started walking toward Dizengoff Street. As I got away from the big hotels, the shops became smaller and more interesting, filled with high-end clothing and funky shoes. I passed several restaurants and bars crowded with fashionably dressed people.

When I arrived, the café was half empty and Andrew wasn't there. I couldn't decide if I was disappointed or relieved. The café was long and narrow, with a bar along one side and a few tables at the very front next to a microphone and chair on a small stage. I took a seat at the back of the bar and ordered a salad and a beer. The bartender wore a halter top with spaghetti straps and pants so sheer I could see the outline of her thong. She had nice shoulders.

I remembered the feeling of rubbing my bare shoulder against my cheek on hot nights. I used to own a great pair of wide-leg pants. They rode low on the hips, showing just a hint of skin—sexy, but not slutty. I sighed and adjusted my skirt. I wasn't dressed too badly: a long straight skirt, cute sandals, my plaid rockabilly blouse with the rosette buttons. At least I'd brought my funky sun hat, a 1930s cloche style with a big flower over one ear. Sheila had found it for me in a thrift store.

The bar filled up, and I started to feel out of place. Everyone was so much older, and I felt shabby in my skirt and blouse compared to the girls in their strappy tank tops and tight jeans. I watched in amazement as this guy kissed a girl hello and gave her bare shoulder a squeeze. She ran her hands through the guy's hair, laughing. I felt shocked. It had been so long since I'd seen people casually touching each other.

I was about to leave when Andrew came in. He was wearing jeans, his sunglasses pushed up on top of his head, making his hair spike up. My stomach tightened when I saw him. He settled his guitar case by the bar and leaned in to kiss the bartender. I couldn't hear what they were saying because a woman in a red dress and red highlights was singing a Hebrew pop song. Andrew stood at the bar near the stage drinking a beer. He didn't see me. Then a couple in matching Mao military hats sang "No Woman, No Cry." The audience joined in. Everyone in the bar seemed to know each other.

They clapped one another on the back and exchanged kisses.

I moved closer to the wall by the bar. After a few more songs Andrew got up and sang "Crazy." I liked the way he tilted his hips forward to support his guitar. The bar made me think of playing with the Neon DayGlos, the excitement of Flip counting us in to play "Walking After Midnight." I could feel the cowboy boots on my feet, see the spiderweb tattoo on Matt's biceps. *And a one and a two.* The low twang of the banjo sang out under my fingers.

Andrew caught my eye as he came off the stage and headed over to me. I twisted my skirt between my fingers.

"You came."

"I shouldn't have."

"Why not?"

I shrugged. "I liked the songs you played." I wanted to run my fingers through his hair, have him squeeze my shoulder.

"So, guitar girl, if you were up there, what would you play?"

I tilted my head to the side. "Maybe some Carter Family or an Alison Krauss song."

"I'd like to hear you. Any chance you'd get up tonight?"

"Nah, I don't think so."

"Oh, c'mon. I bet you're great. I heard you sing the other day."

"Well…"

A guy with reddish hair wearing baggy shorts and a T-shirt clapped Andrew on the back. "Great set, dude."

Andrew turned toward the guy. "Thanks."

"Hey, I want you to meet some people." Before Andrew could introduce me, the guy was herding him toward a table of his friends.

"I'll catch you later."

"Sure."

Andrew moved off to shake hands with a dyed blond in a cute sundress. His friend with the reddish hair had his arm around another girl.

I checked my watch. It was already 8:30 and unless I was going to take a shared taxi back to Jerusalem, I'd have to leave now to make it before curfew. The doors of the yeshiva locked at 10:00 PM. I took a last look around the bar. It was just like the bar where I used to play: the casual hookups, the guys checking you out. I could almost taste the flat combination of beer and cigarettes flavoring Matt's mouth. It was the taste of disappointment. Right. I was done with that.

I finished my drink and slipped out of the bar into the warm Tel Aviv night and started walking to the bus stop.

&EIGHT

There were no classes at the yeshiva Friday morning so Aviva and I slept in. We spent the morning cleaning our room and shopping at the grocery store in French Hill. In the afternoon I gave Aviva a guitar lesson. When she tired of practicing, she went to talk to some friends, leaving me with the guitar. I played some of the new Jewish songs I'd learned, and then I found my fingers playing the *Abbey Road* medley the guitarists had played on the rooftop of the hostel. I thought about Andrew playing "Crazy" in the bar in Tel Aviv. When Aviva asked what I'd done the night before, I told her I'd gone out with Michelle. She'd yawned and said she'd gone to Israeli dancing. I was relieved she didn't ask for details.

In the afternoon, Aviva and I went to stay overnight for Shabbos with Aviva's cousins, Dan and Leah.

THE BOOK OF TREES

They lived on the outskirts of French Hill. When I walked into their apartment, I couldn't stop staring at the fabulous view of the Judean Desert from their living-room window.

Dan had already left for *shul* by the time we got there, so Aviva and I helped Leah in the kitchen. Leah had a pretty face with a sprinkling of freckles across her nose, but she wore a head covering like an oversized sock over every single hair on her head, and a giant apron dress over her enormous pregnant belly. I noticed she wore white socks so not even her ankles or feet were exposed. I curled my toes in my sandals to hide my polished pink toenails.

Aviva set the table and I made a fruit salad while Leah rattled off her list of baby worries. Would her mother arrive in time for the baby's birth? What if Leah didn't understand the doctors and nurses at the hospital? Dan and Leah had moved to Israel a year ago. On the counter by the phone was an open notebook with a list of questions written in Hebrew and their English translations. *I am in pain. Please give me an epidural. Please call my mother!*

Leah couldn't imagine how she'd manage the holidays with a newborn in the fall. I couldn't imagine having a baby, period. Aviva seemed enthralled with Leah's pregnant belly. She put her hands on Leah's stomach and even whispered, "Hello, little baby." She was already offering to babysit.

When I finished making the salad, Leah and Aviva were still discussing bassinets and high chairs.

Leah finished wiping down the counters and came to sit with Aviva and me at the table. We each had a glass of juice.

"So"—Leah looked at me—"Aviva told me this is your first trip to Israel. Are you loving it?"

"Yes. I can't wait to explore. We're supposed to go on some trips soon."

"We're going to Massada in a couple of weeks, and then there's a night hike at the end of the month," Aviva said.

Through the kitchen window I could see the desert, pink in the fading evening light. "I'd like to be out there right now." I pointed to the sunset.

"Too hot," Aviva said.

"And dry," Leah added. "I feel parched just looking out there. Ugh." She drank the rest of her juice and got up from the table.

Leah went to pray in the bedroom, and Aviva headed for the spare bedroom with her prayer book, leaving me in the sparsely furnished living room. The couches had been pushed to the side of the room against a bookshelf filled with Talmudic volumes to make space for the dining table. Elaborate silver candlesticks stood next to mismatched silverware and cheap dishes.

What was Andrew doing right now? Drinking with friends? Clubbing in Tel Aviv? I tried to imagine him all scrubbed up for Shabbos, wearing a *kippah*. I suppressed a giggle.

I flopped onto the faded gray couch. I wanted to sing the psalms to welcome the Shabbos queen the way I had at Aviva's parents' house, praying together to create the divine presence of God, not speed-reading through the prayers the way Leah and Aviva were. When I sang alone, I was just one lonely voice, but at school when we all sang together, we created the feeling of God.

I stood up and wandered out to the balcony. The heat overwhelmed me after the air-conditioned apartment. I stood quietly observing the desert hills. Dan and Leah's apartment was at the edge of the city. If you crossed the road, you'd really be in the desert. The sun had gone down and the sky at the horizon was a dreamy swath of pinks and blues.

I imagined the desert like a giant empty plate, a place so big it would obliterate all thought. It wouldn't matter what music you liked or how you dressed. I wouldn't be thinking about Andrew or the trees. I'd just be a body moving in a space, motivated by physical sensations: thirst, hunger, heat, exhaustion. If you were surrounded by nothing but sand, were you still the same person or would the landscape change you?

I shook my head and thought about standing in that huge wide-open space. I couldn't even envision it; it felt too big to fit in my head. I'd be swallowed up in the vastness.

I closed my eyes and started humming one of the Friday-night psalms. *"Yedid Nefesh, Av harahaman."* Soulmate, loving God. I pretended I was singing with a bunch of other people, and I tried to conjure the feeling of Shabbos calm, of God's presence.

Leah came into the living room to light Shabbos candles. She offered Aviva and me little tea lights in glass holders so we could say the blessing. I wondered if I should sing along with them, but before I could decide, Leah whispered the blessing, without looking at us, and then went back to the kitchen. I sang the blessing alone.

Then Dan came in calling, *"Shabbat Shalom."* He was a young guy with a big barrel chest and a brown scruffy beard. We gathered at the table for the blessing of the wine and then we washed our hands. Dan said *hamotzi,* the prayer over the bread, and passed everyone a warm, ripped-off chunk of *challah.* Then Leah brought in the food, and Dan and Leah started discussing the week's Torah portion.

Leah passed me a platter of chicken. "I always think it's crazy Moshe never got to enter the holy land."

"He made a mistake." Dan helped himself to rice.

"But everyone makes mistakes," Leah said.

Shit. I had been swimming in Tel Aviv and chasing Andrew instead of learning the week's Torah portion. "So, what's the story of the week?" I tried to keep my tone light.

Conversation stopped. Aviva raised her eyebrows at me. My cheeks grew hot. "I missed class yesterday," I mumbled.

Dan took a sip of wine. "The Jews enter Israel after wandering in the desert for forty years, but Moshe isn't allowed to enter because he doubted God."

I knew Moshe was Moses, but I didn't know this story. "How did God know Moses doubted him?"

Aviva explained. "God told Moses to strike this rock with his stick to get water. And Moses hesitated a moment, which shows he doubted God."

"Poor Moshe," Leah said. "Such a good guy, and never rewarded for all his trouble. The plagues, the forty years in the desert." She sighed.

"No." Dan smacked the table with his fist. "Moshe was a leader, a role model for the other Jews. He had to be made an example."

I wondered why we were reading this section now. Shouldn't it be read just after Passover in the spring? "Is that the end of the chapter?" I asked. "They go to Israel, but Moses doesn't?" Could I sound any more ignorant? I really needed to read the whole bible this summer, or at least Genesis and Exodus.

Aviva helped herself to more salad. "They get to Israel and they make war on the Ammonites who live there, and they win and resettle the land."

Whoa. "They got there and there were other people, so they just killed them?"

"It was a war," Aviva said.

"It wasn't just a war." Dan waved his fork. "It was our promised land. Of course we would win."

I frowned. You just kill the people who get in your way? I hadn't thought about the trees in the last few days. I'd been too focused on Andrew. Now they came rushing back to my mind. No wonder the trees didn't bother my religious friends. They were probably used to reading about violence in the Torah. I opened my mouth and closed it without speaking.

"Were you going to say something?" Leah asked.

"Uh, no."

"The Torah is full of bloodshed," Dan continued. "Our people's history has been difficult."

"The military is a reality here." Leah patted her rounded tummy. "Our little one will serve."

"Doesn't that bother you?" I felt vaguely nauseated.

"It's a privilege," Dan said.

"Better to fight than be frightened." Leah folded her napkin.

"Or have to hide," Aviva added. I stared at Aviva. Did she really agree with them?

Dan helped himself to a second helping of chicken. "Besides, he'll be fighting for *Eretz Yisrael,* the land of Israel."

"Amen!" Leah raised her wine and clinked her glass against Dan's.

I shifted uncomfortably in my chair.

Dan looked at me and smiled. "Mia, I love all people, I really do." He put his huge hand over his heart. "But it's like your family. If your brother, God forbid, is hurt, you're going to rescue him before any stranger. These"—he gestured with an outstretched arm, suggesting all of Jerusalem—"are my people. Moshe and the Jews had to think of themselves before the Ammonites."

I nodded and pretended to smile. I wanted to leave their apartment immediately. Who else did the Torah say to kill? I felt like I'd gone to see a movie billed as a romantic comedy and it turned out to be a bloody war epic. Why was everyone so accepting of, even excited by, all this violence? It was crazy. I stared at Leah. Was she really okay with her kids growing up to be soldiers? Who were these people?

After dinner Aviva cornered me in the kitchen. "How come you weren't at your Torah class?"

"Oh, that. Right, well. I stayed late at volunteering."

Aviva hesitated a moment and then nodded.

⫷

Shabbos morning we went to Dan and Leah's *shul*. In the afternoon Dan and Leah lay down for a nap. Aviva sat next to me on the balcony, reading a novel. I found a bible in Dan and Leah's living room and flipped through to the section about the Ammonites.

I read for a while, and then I closed the book and looked out over the desert. No wonder the army could plant trees over Arab villages or knock down Arab houses. It was in the Torah; modern Israel fulfilled biblical prophecy. I felt sick to my stomach.

I shuddered and leaned my head back. I couldn't stay with these people any longer. Aviva and I were supposed to hang out until Shabbos ended—five more hours. I tapped my feet on the concrete patio and twisted in the hard plastic lawn chair. I stood up abruptly. "I think I'm going to get going."

Aviva looked up sleepily. "Huh?"

"I feel kinda anxious to go home. I think I'll just head back to the dorm."

Aviva sat up. "You're going to walk in this heat?"

"I'll be okay."

"What should I tell Dan and Leah?"

"Oh, just tell them I felt sick or something."

I quickly retreated from the balcony, leaving Aviva staring after me.

Down on the street, the sun scorched the pavement, but I felt relieved. I walked down the hill toward the Hyatt Hotel. Four o'clock Saturday afternoon and no one knew where I was. I wondered what Andrew was doing. Playing guitar? Drinking a beer? A slightly exhilarated feeling took over me. Too bad it was Shabbos and I could only get places on foot. I stopped in the shade of a bus stop to look at the view. Below me stretched East Jerusalem and then the Old City. The Dome of the Rock gleamed in the midday sun. What if you were Palestinian and you fled in 1948 and you never got to come back and see this view again? My heart felt pinched, imagining it.

Why hadn't I ever jogged through East Jerusalem? Even the bus from downtown took a circuitous route through West Jerusalem. Was East Jerusalem really that dangerous? It didn't look that way from here. I fished in my backpack for my map. I studied the streets and then stuck the map in my pocket. I hesitated a moment. Aviva would have a fit if she knew I walked there, yet I wanted to see what it was like. I'd head straight down to the Old City, just to check things out. I took a swig from my water bottle and headed downhill.

East Jerusalem's quiet streets of apartment blocks and high-fenced buildings had an unkempt, shabby appearance. A thin dog missing patches of fur followed me for a block before disappearing into an abandoned lot. Pink and yellow plastic bags snagged the fences and clung to the corridor of the road like icing on a dry cake. I stopped at a rough-looking gas station, unsure which way to go. Around me buses spewed exhaust. I stood looking down the road, trying to get my bearings. I fumbled in my pocket for my map, but I was reluctant to take it out. Two small boys stared at me and a group of young men looked me up and down suspiciously. There were no women around. Did these guys' families lose their villages? I wanted to say, Sorry, it wasn't me who did it.

I looked nervously around again, crossed my fingers and decided to turn the corner. I hurried along a road without a sidewalk, praying it was the right way. Once this city had belonged to those young men's fathers, and now it didn't. I couldn't imagine how that felt. I walked quickly, without looking back, until I arrived at a more familiar part of the city, not far from Damascus Gate.

Sweat meandered between my breasts and dampened the waistband of my underwear. The sun bore down, fiery on my forearms. Now what? I could walk by Andrew's hostel and see if he was there. What I really wanted was a pool. Last week I'd walked over to the King David Hotel and had ice tea in the lobby. I'd stared at the swimmers enjoying the water. Surely there was a women's swim club somewhere. Or maybe I could pretend to be someone else, just for an hour, and strip off my modest sundress and plunge into the water. I used to own the cutest aqua bikini with little bows at the hips. I sat down at a bus stop and flipped through the pages of my guidebook to look for a hotel, the fancier the better.

The streets were deserted except for a young religious guy across the street in a black hat, black jacket and white shirt. I saw him look at me and then quickly look away. I guessed he was bored on Shabbos and out for a walk too. I tried to ignore him and concentrate on my map. When I looked up, I saw the guy's dick jutting out of his pants. Sick. I jammed my guidebook in my bag and ran several long hot blocks until I came to the American Colony Hotel.

Dust swirled around a young Arab boy selling fruit juice in front of the hotel. Where did he live? Then I stopped in the entranceway of the hotel and gazed at the stone walls, the elegant greenery, the mosaic floors. At the far end of the hall an archway led to a tranquil pool. There was also a small bookstore. The desk clerk eyed me. I strolled right past him.

I walked down the hallway to the pool, sat in the shade of an umbrella and kicked off my sandals. I felt cooler just looking at the water. A waiter came by and I ordered an ice tea, which you're probably not supposed to do on Shabbos, but I could wait until sundown to pay for it. That was okay, wasn't it?

NINE

One of my Bubbie Bess's friends, who had moved to Israel to be near her kids, called me up and invited me out to tea. Mrs. Shanowitz used to have the lawn chair next to Bubbie Bess at her Florida condo.

"I'll take you somewhere where it won't feel like Israel. Meet me at Ticho House." Only a few blocks away from Zion Square, Ticho House was nestled in a rich green garden with a shady café patio.

I wasn't sure why I agreed. I'd never really liked Mrs. Shanowitz. She was a busybody who always said you looked either too thin or too fat. She always had a nice boy she wanted to set you up with, someone who was going to be a lawyer or had just got into Yale. I only agreed to meet her because her voice reminded me of Bubbie Bess.

Mrs. Shanowitz wore closed-toe shoes despite the heat and the same kind of white polyester pants with a sharp crease down the front and giant sunglasses that Bubbie Bess liked to wear. A huge diamond sparkled like a chandelier on her left hand.

Mrs. Shanowitz gave me two noisy kisses, one on each cheek, and then peppered me with questions about Sheila and Flip. I felt briefly homesick for my family, listening to her accent. She said *gas* the way Bess said it—*gaz*—as if she was speaking French.

She ordered tea and started complaining. Israel was too hot, too dirty, too dangerous. Still, she couldn't afford another broken hip from the ice at home. Her health insurance made Florida too expensive. She couldn't go gallivanting to see the sights because the uneven Jerusalem stone on the roads and sidewalks might trip her. Her children were too busy with their own lives and didn't have time to ferry her around.

I tuned her out and drank in the tall trees at the edge of the garden. Don would like to sit under those.

"I've only been to the Wall once since I came here," Mrs. Shanowitz said.

"Would you like to go now?"

"Oh, I'm a little tired. It's so hot."

"We could take a cab."

"If it's not too much trouble." She looked pleased.

The cab driver took us to Dung Gate, where the tour buses let off tourists close to the *Kotel*. I helped

Mrs. Shanowitz across the plaza and to a chair by the wall. I sat a few rows back. It was mid-afternoon and very hot. Tourists thronged the wall, gawking at the stones instead of praying. I sighed. A wall, people, a symbol. And me? I was sick of thinking about it.

Mrs. Shanowitz didn't pray; she people-watched. After a few minutes she asked to walk around. She held tightly on to my arm and kept up a steady commentary. "Christians, hmm. I can't imagine what they get out of all this, but I suppose they're curious. Do you think they could have restricted times? Oh, I guess that would be unpopular. Wow, look at the size of the men's side. So much bigger. I guess that's religion for you, squishing the women off in a corner. Oh, I hope I haven't insulted a nice girl like you. Oh good. That goes to show."

When we got back to the gate, I stuck Mrs. Shanowitz in a taxi.

"I'm going to send Bess a card and tell her how delicious you are." She squeezed my shoulder. "You keep safe. No riding on buses or wandering alone. Okay then." She planted more rose-scented kisses on my cheeks, and then I closed the taxi door.

I tried to wipe the smell of old-lady perfume off me as I climbed the stairs back up to the balcony overlooking the plaza and the *Kotel*. Tourists strolled across the ancient stones, others prayed at the wall, the Dome glinting in the background. I'd seen pictures of the first soldiers to arrive at the wall when it was recaptured in '67.

They were the first Jews to get there in centuries. The pictures made me feel like crying, as if hands were squeezing my chest. I couldn't imagine the city without the *Kotel*. Yet how many Ammonites or Palestinians had to be killed to get it? I kept wondering, had the Israeli army killed Palestinians because they'd read in the bible that the Jews had killed the Ammonites? Did it make it easier?

I'd tried to explore other Arab parts of the city since my walk through East Jerusalem. I'd wandered down a street full of Arab cafés and falafel stands near Damascus Gate and seen the lines of people outside the Ministry of Justice. I'd stopped at a corner store to ask for a café recommendation from a teenage boy snacking on a bag of sunflower seeds. He thought about it for a moment, called out in Arabic toward the back of the shop and was joined by three other boys. They conferred and wrote down several names for me. "We go together?" asked the oldest. I hesitated and said, 'No, thank you," as politely as I could. I'd wandered by the cafés but didn't go in because there were only men in them. The only women I'd noticed were two old women sitting cross-legged, selling baskets of leafy green vegetables in front of a shoe shop on King David Street. They looked out of place in their headscarves on the busy road.

I walked away from the *Kotel* through the narrow Old City streets to the Armenian section. I hadn't let myself go near Andrew's hostel, not even to play guitar or just say hi. Now I needed to talk to him again. Besides, I was so close to the hostel, it would be rude not to stop by. I'd just say hello and then I'd get up and go. Maybe they'd be playing guitar again.

As I rounded the corner to the hostel, I saw Andrew sitting in the open lobby playing backgammon with the guy who'd pulled him away from me in the bar in Tel Aviv. I felt my cheeks flush.

Andrew looked up. "Long time no see. Where ya been?"

"Oh, just around. Busy, you know."

He nodded to his backgammon partner. "This is my buddy, Kyle."

Kyle gave me a knowing smile and held out his hand. "I've heard about you."

My cheeks burned.

Andrew jumped up. "Mia's not one for shaking hands."

"Sweaty palms?"

"Not at all." I took a swig of water and eyed Kyle from above my water bottle. I didn't like the way he looked me over.

"Do you wanna join us for a drink?" Kyle pointed to a seat.

"I'm interrupting your game." I turned to go.

"Oh, we were done anyway." Andrew moved a few pieces off the board and gave me a cocky smile.

Kyle coughed.

Andrew got up. "Let's go upstairs."

I looked down and tried to ignore Kyle's leering smile.

"So, what have you been up to?" Andrew turned to look at me as we climbed the stairs.

"I've been busy with school."

"You never came back to play music. One of the guys was asking about you. He liked your voice."

"Well, you know, religious girls shouldn't really be hanging out and all. I've been trying to concentrate on my studies."

Andrew stopped by a door and grinned. "So, why are you here?"

"Oh, I was just walking by…"

"And?"

"I'm still thinking about those trees. I wanted your opinion…"

Andrew unlocked the door. "Here okay?"

"Um, well." I peered into the narrow room. Next to the unmade bed was a wooden table and chair. In the corner of the room, a purple and green backpack spilled clothes beside Andrew's guitar. I envisioned us lying in that unmade bed. *Get up and go, Mia. Just leave. Or at least talk to him on the roof. Say you're uncomfortable in his room.* I felt myself pulled toward that bed like a magnet. "Yeah, sure. This is fine." I left the door open.

Andrew cleared the chair for me and sat down on the bed. "So?"

I clasped my hands behind my back. "I'm still thinking about those trees, the JNF forests."

Andrew tapped his fingers on his bare knees. "It takes up a lot of brain space, doesn't it?"

I nodded. He leaned back against the wall and spread his hands, palms up, on his lap, listening. I took a deep breath. "The trees, they're freaking me out, because once I learned about them, I thought, Oh, well there must be a difference between the Israeli government, which isn't perfect, and the Torah, the Bible, which is."

"You mean a gap between ideal and reality?"

"Yeah, exactly. Like the Torah is the ideal, and then Israel is the reality, and they don't match up. And I thought, I'm okay with that. But I've been reading the Torah and listening to people at school talk, and I'm not sure the Torah is so ideal either."

Andrew gave me an amused smile. I tried to ignore it. Who cared if I sounded like a kid? "I don't think I agree that this land was given just to the Jews," I said. "That sounds so exclusionary."

"That's kind of what religion is about, excluding others."

"I thought it was about peace and love." I could see Andrew suppressing a grin. Shit, I hated sounding so stupid. I dug my fingers into my arms. "What's the point of being religious if it's not about helping others? The ten commandments and all that. Thou shalt not kill."

"And yet the Jews do."

I caught my breath. He was right. "And so do the Palestinians."

"That's true too."

We sat quietly for a moment as I tried to take in everything we'd said. I wished I was taking notes so I could absorb the different ideas. Andrew sighed and ran his hands through his hair. He looked more serious than I'd ever seen him. Then he stretched his arms over his head and I caught a glimpse of his armpit hair peeking out of the sleeve of his T-shirt. I looked down at my hands.

I took another breath and looked back up at Andrew. "Sometimes I wish I believed in Israel a little more."

"Whaddya mean?"

"I guess I mean, I wish I really believed a Jewish homeland was worth all the bloodshed."

Andrew narrowed his eyes. "Do you really want to believe that?"

I shrugged. "I'm not sure. My roommate does." I rubbed my eyes and stared out the window. "I think maybe they all do, at my school. It's freaking me out. I'm, like, the only one who doesn't." I looked back at Andrew. "I feel so guilty criticizing Israel. You're the only person I can talk to about these things." I clenched my hands behind my back. It sounded so intimate.

Andrew raised one eyebrow, which sent little shivers across my skin. We sat for a moment, not talking. I tried not to think about how good he smelled.

Andrew yawned. "I have to go to work soon."

"At the museum?"

"Yes." He stood and picked up his towel.

"Oh, I'll go now."

"No, stay. We can walk to the bus stop together."

I could feel myself glowing: he wanted to walk with me. Andrew left the room with a towel, soap and some clothes.

I sighed and let my elbows rest on my knees, my chin propped in my hands. On the table lay a guidebook, a diary with a map on the cover, and a copy of *The Hitchhiker's Guide to the Galaxy*. Andrew's toothbrush and toothpaste, a handful of change, his sunglasses and sunscreen and a tube of deodorant sat next to the books. On the back of the chair dangled a red and white bandanna, stiff with sweat. I picked it up, put it back on the chair and then picked it up again and brought it to my face. I allowed myself one little sniff, then another, until my face was buried in the cloth and I was inhaling deeply. It smelled both sweet and salty. A sensation of falling came over me. Lights flashed behind my closed eyelids, like when I was a kid and I pressed on my lids while looking up at the sky on a sunny day. It was as if I had found something I didn't know I was looking for, but now that I had seen it—or smelled it—I thought maybe it should have been my quest all along.

Footsteps sounded in the hallway and Andrew appeared neatly dressed in khakis and a collar shirt. I shoved the bandanna in my pocket.

"You ready to go?"

"Oh, okay." I got up. He stood waiting in the doorway. "Now?"

"Yes."

I picked up my backpack. The bandanna bulged in my pocket. Andrew rummaged through some papers on the corner of the table. My hand went to sneak the bandanna back, but he was already turning to me.

"Here." He held out a scrap of paper.

"What's this?"

"It's the name of this book Sonia recommended to me. It's about the Palestinians, the *Nakba*."

"Oh, okay. Yeah, that would be good." I nodded. The *Nakba*. I was too embarrassed to ask what it meant.

At the bus stop, I said, "I'm going to walk up to the bookstore, the one where you used to play."

"You won't find that book at the Steimatsky's on Ben Yehuda. Sonia said you have to go to the bookstore at the American Colony Hotel."

"Oh, thanks." I started walking away and then changed my mind. "Hey, you're not playing on Ben Yehuda anymore?"

"No."

"Why not?"

Andrew rubbed his forehead. "It's complicated. I found other things to do."

"Like?"

He shook his head. "It's too long a story to tell you now."

"Oh."

"I'll call you."

I frowned. "No, you can't do that." I imagined the girls hovering over the phone in the lounge. *Mia, who's calling? Mia, who's the guy with the sexy voice on the phone?* It'd be all over the dorm in moments.

"Then how can I find you?"

A little thrill ran through me. He wanted to find me. "You can't."

He smiled. "I'm just supposed to wait like… "

I laughed. "Like some teenage girl?"

"Yeah, like some teenage girl." He widened his stance, one hand on his hip.

Andrew's bus pulled up to the stop. I started walking away. "See you around."

Andrew shook his finger at me.

I watched his bus pull away. I could tell everyone I was going to visit long-lost cousins in Tel Aviv for the weekend. I could sneak away for an afternoon and meet Andrew at the beach and…what? We'd walk in the waves and hold hands and kiss and then maybe…my mind raced. I was naked in his arms. I was sniffing his neck for more of that delicious scent. We would make slow, sensual love, and then I'd take his T-shirt back to the dorm. While all the other girls were sleeping in their single beds, thinking their pristine thoughts about their *b'shert*, their one true love, I'd be writhing in Andrew's T-shirt.

This was *so* not why I was supposed to be in Israel.

Why weren't the other girls meeting hot guys like Andrew? Was I the only one not getting off on Israeli dancing and volunteer work? I was a slut at heart, that had to be it. Now I knew why everyone warned me against wandering around the city: bombs weren't dangerous, men were. No, not men. It was me. I was dangerous. I felt a little chill run down my spine. Hadn't I always wanted to be dangerous? No, that was the Old Mia. The New Mia was supposed to be pious and do good deeds. I hugged my arms around myself. I couldn't help it; I just wanted to be with Andrew.

I fingered the paper Andrew had handed me. Sheila had given me money to buy something special for myself. The other yeshiva girls bought beautiful pottery matchboxes for their Shabbos candles, or necklaces with their name written on a grain of rice, not books about the *Nakba*.

I walked around the Old City, up Shivtei Yisrael Street, which bisected the ultra-religious community of Mea She'arim from East Jerusalem to the American Colony Hotel. In the little bookstore I handed the clerk the scrap of paper with the book title Andrew had recommended. The clerk handed me a paperback entitled *The Nakba*. On the cover was a black-and-white picture of a bulldozer uprooting an olive tree.

I took a bus through East Jerusalem up to French Hill and then walked the rest of the way to the yeshiva.

Back in my dorm room I lay down on my bed with the book. It wasn't like any other Jewish book or article I had read. It was about the *Nakba*, the catastrophe of 600,000 or more Palestinians who were violently expelled from their homes in 1948, who became refugees in their own land, who lost their orange groves, their olive trees, their fresh figs.

I read a poem by Tawfiq Zayyad.

> *I shall carve the record of all my sufferings, and all my*
> *secrets,*
> *On an olive tree, in the courtyard, of the house…*
> *I shall carve the number of each deed of our usurped*
> *land,*
> *The location of my village and its boundaries,*
> *The demolished houses of its people, my uprooted trees…*

I shoved the book off my lap. I could feel the heat of it searing my legs.

I didn't know who came first, whose land it originally was, but I understood that women had lost their houses. I understood men had lost their trees. I understood children had lost their homeland.

By the time Aviva came home, I had a raging headache.

"How was your day?" She put down her bag and flopped on her bed.

I was so wrecked I could barely answer. I mumbled something under my breath.

Aviva turned to look at me. "You don't look okay."

"I've been reading about the *Nakba*." I held up the book.

"The what?"

"The Palestinian expulsion."

"The Palestinian what?"

"It's what the Palestinians call what happened to them in 1948, after the war."

"I thought they all just fled. What are you reading that for anyway?"

"A friend recommended it. I've been thinking about those trees we saw at the retreat, the ones that are planted where there used to be a village."

"That really got to you, didn't it?"

"Aviva, people lost their villages, their homes, their trees, their lives. I can't imagine what that must be like."

"It happened to the Jews time after time. Pogroms, the Holocaust..."

"And so you think that justifies taking over Palestinian land by force?"

"No, no. I'm not saying that at all." Aviva sat up and gripped the edge of her mattress. "I'm saying you can't please everyone. This is the Jewish homeland. The Palestinians should have gone to some other Arab country."

"But they lived here. They still do, apparently." I let my head drop into my hands and shook it from side to side.

"Why are you so upset?"

I took a deep breath. "I want Jews to be free and have a homeland, but not if it means killing other people to do it."

Aviva stood up and gave me a hug. "Mia, you have such a big heart."

I resisted the urge to wrestle out of her embrace.

Aviva turned back to her desk and started stacking her books into a pile. "It's not like it's any different at home. All of North America used to belong to the native people until the Europeans showed up."

"But that's different."

"How so?"

"I don't know." I felt like shouting at her. I stood up and walked to the door.

"Where are you going?"

"For a walk. I need...I need some air."

"I thought we were going to make dinner together."

"Yeah, I don't think I'm hungry. I'll see you later." I shoved the book into my desk drawer and ran out of the room. I resisted slamming the door behind me. The sun was setting and I shouldn't have been walking alone at night. I didn't care.

The next morning Michelle and I sat with our books open at our desk. I tried to follow along with her reading, but my eyes kept drifting to the view of the street from the window. How old was the road? Did Palestinian people build it or was it a new Israeli street?

"Mia?" Michelle tapped the table between our open books.

I looked up. "Huh?"

"I asked if you wanted to read."

"Oh, sure."

"You're not on the right page."

"Sorry, it flipped over." I smoothed the page open.

Michelle rolled her eyes. "Okay, so it says to build a table of acacia wood two cubits in length, a cubit in width and a cubit and a half in height."

I scanned the page with my index finger. "Right."

"You're still on the wrong section. What's wrong with you?"

"I'm just…distracted."

Michelle frowned. "I've noticed."

"Can you go on without me?"

Relief showed across Michelle's face. "Sure."

"I'll catch up with you later." I bolted from the table and took the stairs two at a time out of the building to the bus stop. I'd started to read the second part of the

Nakba book during break and my mind was reeling. When I got to Andrew's hostel, I raced up the stairs and banged on his door.

"C'mon in."

I burst in, breathing hard, sweat streaking my face and forming circles under the arms of my shirt. Andrew sat bare-chested in his bed with his guitar. "Oh." I stopped, backing out of the room. I couldn't help gazing at his naked chest. His body was as I imagined—hairless and muscular without being brawny. Oh God, what was I doing here? "Can you get dressed?" I blurted out.

"You burst in and expect clothing?"

I stepped back. "I…" Shit, I thought, I shouldn't be here. But who the hell else could I talk to?

Andrew smiled. "Just give me a second." I closed the door and a moment later he called out, "Okay, come in."

I stepped back into the room, waving the book in my hand. Andrew had put on a T-shirt. "So, here's what I don't get. Why don't I know about this?"

"Shouldn't you be in class?"

"I couldn't concentrate. How can I not know any of this?"

"Because you've been brainwashed by Zionists. Why would you know?"

I shoved some clothes off his chair and sat down. "We have to go to Liberty Bell Park."

"Now?"

"Right now."

"Why?"

"Because you know the beautiful olive trees, those gorgeous olives in the garden for Martin Luther King Junior?"

"Yeah?"

"C'mon, I'll tell you there."

Outside I hailed a cab. I didn't have the patience for more buses.

The cab let us out at the edge of the sprawling green lawns of the park. I strode across the grass, past the bell, toward a grove of gnarled old olive trees where I had walked a few weeks before. "Here, you see these gorgeous trees? You see them? This book"—I brandished it—"it's like this huge secret. Do people not know about it or do they know and not care? They only hear about the terrorist attacks."

"So why are we here?"

"Oh, well apparently these all didn't just grow here. Some were taken from Palestinian lands and dedicated to Martin Luther King Junior How fucked up is that? Can you imagine if King had known trees were stolen in his honor? It wasn't enough for the Israelis to plant their own trees on Palestinian land. They had to steal Palestinian trees too. It's like they didn't really have an identity, so they had to plant it, and when that wasn't good enough, they had to steal someone else's." I was breathing hard, yelling, my face puffed up and red. "I feel…rocked. I feel so stupid."

Andrew held out a hand to stop me. "It's not so black and white. Terrorists still kill people."

I took his hand without thinking and squeezed it hard. "And can you blame them? I can't imagine anything but more violence."

"You are really strong."

I stopped squeezing his hand and realized we were touching. I felt my cheeks flame. My pulse was racing. "There are so many things I just don't know."

"Yes."

"I don't know where to start learning, or how to think. The more I think, the more confused I am." I got up and started walking. "I can't sit still. I need to get out of here. Let's get something to drink."

We walked over to Emek Refaim, Andrew struggling to keep up with my frenzied pace. By the time we got there, some of my anger had fizzled. My T-shirt stuck to my back and my hair felt stiff with dried sweat under my sun hat. I gulped down two ice teas. We sat in silence, just looking out at the cars and people going by. When I finished my second drink, I turned to Andrew. "You know why I became religious?"

"Why?"

"I wanted the world spelled out clearly for me. I wanted clear lines of right and wrong."

Andrew nodded. "It's never—"

"Don't say a thing," I said fiercely.

I rubbed my eyes to stop tears from forming. Andrew talked a little about an Israeli guy he met at the museum who played bass. They were thinking about getting together for a jam session. I nodded, pretending to be interested. I gazed out the window and absently started counting cars.

"Mia?" Andrew tapped his fingers on my wrist.

I looked down at his hand, touching me, and then at my watch. "I'm supposed to be back at school for prayers."

"Are you going to go?"

I looked out at the darkening sky. "No, I don't think so." Evening prayers were optional.

I went to the bathroom and washed my face, trying to get the tight sweaty feeling off my skin. I felt exhausted, as if my anger had depleted my energy.

When I got back to the table, Andrew stood up. "Come. Let's go for a walk."

Outside, the side streets were quiet. I tried not to think about the trees or the *Nakba* or what it meant to be a Jew in a country that was your own and not your own. How lucky, how plagued. Our shoulders brushed as we walked down the street, and I briefly felt the heat of Andrew's skin through my T-shirt. Goose bumps ran down my arms. I wanted to lay my head against his shoulder and have him take all my pain away.

"I've been meaning to ask you something," I said.

"Yeah?" He raised one eyebrow over his sunglasses. I felt myself quake a little.

"Why don't you play on Ben Yehuda anymore?"

Andrew sighed and his shoulders shrank into his T-shirt. "It's just not what I'm supposed to do."

I nodded, as if I understood. "I mean," I tried again, "why did you play in the first place?"

"It was what I was supposed to do."

I faced him. "You mean your quest?"

Andrew stopped and looked at me over his sunglasses. His sharp eyes pierced into me and I felt my heart beat a little faster. "No, my responsibility." He suddenly looked older and sadder. I could see lines around his eyes.

We had wandered back into the park. Children jumped on a giant trampoline and rode a mini Ferris wheel in a small fairground beyond the trees. When had the rides appeared? Had they been in the park earlier? I noticed a cotton-candy vendor. A huge reddish half-disk of a moon descended rapidly toward the horizon.

"You know, I've never seen the moon set before. I never knew it did, until I got here. Why were you supposed to sing on Ben Yehuda?"

"I just had this feeling I had to sing where people could hear. I didn't think I was a prophet or anything. I mean, what's the difference between that and being crazy?" Andrew's voice was quieter than before.

We sat down in the grass next to each other. I fought the urge to let my elbow bump against his.

Andrew sat with his knees pulled up to his chest, his sunglasses shoved into his hair. "I had to play certain songs, not for their words, more for their emotion. A certain longing, you know? I had to just play the sadness I felt around here."

"Sadness?"

Andrew was silent a moment. He stared down at his sandals. "My first night here I was in the Russian Compound and terrorists shot up the street outside the bar. Kyle and I hid under a table. It was freaking scary shit. I didn't know what to do about it. So I played what I thought was right."

"You played Patsy Cline's 'Crazy' a lot. I liked that."

"Yeah, I played that and 'Dust in the Wind' and 'Daniel,' and then one day I woke up and I thought, What the hell am I doing? I mean, you thought I was a beggar. So I thought I better do something else."

"Wait."

"What?"

"How did you make that leap?"

"What leap?"

"I mean, how did you decide you had to help?"

The moon swelled as it approached the horizon. Children ran around us, alternating between the Ferris wheel and the giant trampoline. Only Arab children, I realized. I could tell by the parents' clothes. Was it a holiday I hadn't heard of? Had these people lost their homes? What was I doing in a dark park in a strange city listening to Andrew's smooth voice? What lie would I tell Aviva tonight?

"I couldn't be a bystander," he said. "I was reading some articles Sonia lent me, about the way the Israeli army kills innocent bystanders or imprisons innocent people as precautions, or surrounds a community and cuts people off from the supplies they need to survive." Andrew's face had fallen into a tight mask I'd never seen before. His clasped hands were white with tension.

"But why this problem?"

Andrew cracked his knuckles. "Maybe because I had nothing else to do—I didn't have to be anywhere. My mind wasn't clouded with other things, like work or surfing or my mom. Or maybe it was because I wasn't on either side. I could just be neutral."

"And so what did you do?"

"I'm getting to that. So, Sonia sent me on this crazy tour of the West Bank. It's run through a hostel by this Palestinian guy. You go through the checkpoints and it's like going to a third-world country. It's totally different. There's no infrastructure, the economy is practically destroyed because every time they shut the checkpoints, no one works. It's a breeding ground for hate, because how could it be otherwise? At the end we passed by a school and I thought, This is what I have to do next. So that's where I've been the past few weeks, volunteering at this school. I'm teaching music and tutoring in English. I'm also helping rebuild a house next week. The military destroyed this guy's house because it's in the wrong place, and this organization gets volunteers to help rebuild it. You could come too, if you like."

"It sounds dangerous."

"Yeah, maybe. Not as much as other protests."

"Like what?"

"There's a group that supports Palestinians when their homes are threatened. It's a nonviolent protest, but I think it can be dangerous. You know—bulldozers."

"Whoa."

We sat silently in the park. I felt dazed with possibilities. The moon dipped below the horizon and the park got darker. I stood up and stretched my arms above my head. "I should get going."

Andrew stood up and we started walking out of the park. "What about rebuilding that house?"

"What about it?"

"You could come."

"Maybe." I tried to imagine explaining that one to Aviva.

"How can I give you the details without your phone number?"

"I'll find you."

"You're not allowed to have guy friends?"

I sighed. "I'm not even supposed to know any guys."

"Can I tell you something?"

"Sure." I stopped and faced him. For a second I thought he was going to tell me he wanted to kiss me.

And I wanted him to so badly. Forget waiting for the perfect husband. I wanted to feel Andrew's lips on mine, his strong arms around my back.

He said, "Mia, maybe you should stay in your world and enjoy the summer and your studies. Don't let Israel ruin your Israel."

I stopped and stared at him, letting his words sink in. "Don't let Israel ruin your Israel," I repeated. We were at the street now, by the bus stop.

"Yes."

"You don't really think that."

"Do you?"

I hesitated for a moment. "I want everything. I want Israel to be the homecoming I thought it would be, and I want to know the truth. And I'm not hearing it at school."

"No one talks about the occupation at your school?"

"Oh, maybe some do, but girls are here to learn Torah. They're more interested in old books than politics."

"And you?"

"I don't want to wear blinders. Something is being covered up—why the terrorists are attacking—and I want to know the truth."

"And when you find it, what will you do then?"

"I'm not sure."

Andrew nodded.

"Well, see you around."

"Sure, see ya."

I walked away from Andrew through the cool night, the streetlights casting pools of light across the sidewalks. I wasn't ready for the sway of the bus. Tears started to come, slowly at first, then faster, until they were coursing down my face. I wanted to pretend I didn't know about the trees. I wanted Israel to be the perfect Jewish homeland I'd imagined. Now I knew better. I let out a sob.

TEN

I couldn't imagine my Israel experience getting any crazier, but the next day at B'nos Sarah a horde of screaming, hugging, dancing girls mobbed the lounge. In the middle I spotted Chani, her hand outstretched, a sparkling diamond ring on her finger.

Aglow and gushing over her ring, Chani breathlessly described how Yosef had proposed: the flowers, the view of Jerusalem. She alternately cried and laughed, and shrieked that she needed to call home. The other girls whirled around dancing a *horah*, hair flying, shoes squeaking on the linoleum. *Kol sason v'kol simcha, kol chatan v'kol kallah!* The voice of joy and happiness, the voice of the groom and bride. It had been the same for a girl named Rebecca last week, and Sarah the week before. They were all barely twenty-one, if that. I watched the twirling girls. They all seemed so outrageously content with their lives. Maybe if I was more like them, ready to settle down with a nice boy, I'd be happier. I quietly climbed the stairs to my Torah class.

Upstairs, Michelle was waiting for me by the window. Most of the other girls weren't even in the room yet, but Michelle had already begun reading. If she wanted to talk about Chani's engagement, she didn't let on, which was fine by me. We had a routine now. First we skimmed the story in English, and then we painstakingly went through the Hebrew, matching clause for clause, stopping to read the commentaries as we went along. We were up to the story of Noah.

I was confused by the story. Why would God let everyone but Noah drown? Michelle had moved on to the opening Hebrew line. "What do you think 'Noah was perfect in his generation' means? Maybe Rashi has something to say about it." Michelle scanned her Rashi commentary for the corresponding line.

"Wait."

"What?"

"Why do you think God was so angry?"

"The Jews weren't following the laws."

"But killing everyone? What about innocent babies? I mean, surely there must have been other righteous people besides Noah and his family."

"No. According to the story they were all evil."

I opened my mouth and then closed it.

"What?"

I paused. "Doesn't it sound like something people made up after it all happened, to try to understand the flood?"

"What are you talking about?"

"Oh, c'mon. Can't you see it? There's a really bad flood, almost everyone dies, and then they need to make sense of it, so they write this story."

Michelle pressed her lips tightly together. "This is the word of God."

I stared at her. "Yeah, but…"

"It's the word of God, as written by Moshe."

"By Moses? But what about the stuff that came after him?"

"Oh, he knew that too."

I lay my hands flat on the table. "Michelle, don't bullshit me. You don't really believe that."

"I do." She looked beatific.

"Get out of here."

"You don't believe?"

"I mean, it's a beautiful book, a really great creation myth and all, but…"

Michelle's mouth tightened into a taut pucker. "If you don't believe, then why are you here?"

I didn't know what to say. We sat staring at each other. "I like being Jewish and I thought it would be good to learn a little more. I mean, I believe in God, you know, like he's a force around us…"

Michelle looked anxious. She tugged on her hair.

"Oh, well." I waved a hand dismissively in front of my face. "I can pretend it's all true when we study together."

Michelle gave me a doubtful look.

"No, I get it," I continued. "Noah and his family were the only righteous people, and Moses knew it all— past, present, future. Got it." I knew I didn't sound convincing. I secured one of my braids with a bobby pin. "So, what does Rashi have to say?"

Michelle stared at me for another moment and then looked down at her book.

During our class discussion, I listened carefully to the other girls. Like Michelle, they all took the Noah story literally, as if it had really happened. They weren't reading it as some cool myth; they believed it was the Word of God. I knit my hands together and tried to keep from squirming in my chair. I suddenly felt like an alien. No, I'd stumbled into a group of aliens, and I was the normal one. I excused myself from class and went to sit in the lounge. I took a long drink of water. Was this the kind of thing Sheila had been freaking out about? I shook my head. I'd imagined God had giant ears and listened without making judgments or suggestions. You could say, "God, I haven't a clue what I want to do with my life," and he would say, "Huh, I hear you." I thought God was something we could create ourselves, by singing, by praying.

I suddenly knew why I'd never fit in at B'nos Sarah. It wasn't the dating scene or my lack of knowledge or even being secretly in love with Andrew. It wasn't that no one cared about the plight of Palestinians or Israel's human-rights record. The problem was I didn't believe in God the way the rest of the B'nos Sarah girls did. I didn't glow with the light of believing. I hadn't been saved. I peered back into the classroom. I could see the students laughing. I headed up to the roof deck and sat in the shade.

I sighed and looked out over the desert. I imagined standing out there, being so hot, with nothing but the horizon in the distance. I could breathe out all the crazy thoughts in my head about the Torah, about Andrew, about the trees. I'd just be a body in a space, walking, drinking, breathing, being.

Maybe there was a hike I could do myself, nothing too strenuous, but just out there. I could do the hike to Ein Gedi I'd read about in my guidebook, the one with waterfalls.

My next class was starting, but the thought of a chair in the *beit midrash* made my shoulders ache. I didn't want to read about our foremothers and forefathers in the desert. I wanted to *be* in the desert.

I wouldn't go back to class today. I needed to keep moving, to keep my head empty of Andrew, the trees, the B'nos Sarah girls and their beliefs. I walked quickly down the stairs and back to the dorm. A hike in the desert would clear my thoughts. At the end, I could soak in the Ein Gedi waterfalls.

In my room I traded my prayer book for my backpack with a water bottle, a sandwich and a guidebook and headed for the central bus station.

The bus left the busy streets of Jerusalem and descended into dry brown hills. Tire heaps surrounded a cluster of plastic-tarp shacks; goats wandered along the side of the road. Up close the desert was more rocky hills than flat sand.

The bus dropped me off at the side of the highway. I gazed uncertainly at the bus driver. "Here?"

He pointed into the brown expanse of desert.

I felt my guts tighten. "I just start walking?"

Below me the bus rumbled. The other passengers stared out the windows. I saw a soldier roll his eyes.

"Look." The bus driver pointed. "There's the entrance."

I squinted into the glaze of dust and sand and made out a small hut. "Oh." I stepped off the bus and watched it continue into the desert. If I stood on the other side of the road, the bus would eventually come back. I almost did that: just stood there, sipping my water. Who goes hiking alone in the heat of a desert afternoon? I crossed the road and crouched in the dirt.

Up close the desert was a scorched, hot brown. Heat rose from below me, swirling in little gusts. The sun blazed down, burning through the thin layer of my shirt. In the distance I could make out the shimmer of the Dead Sea.

From down the road, a man approached. He wore a tank top and loose cream-colored pants. Over his shoulders spilled a mane of long dark ringlets. He carried an old-fashioned water bottle, the soft-fabric kind, slung over one shoulder. I watched him walk toward me until he stood across the road. He was in his thirties I guessed, dark-skinned and muscular. I noticed he wore thin-soled sandals with narrow straps. He looked into my eyes without smiling, and in heavily Israeli-accented English he said, "We meet in the desert. It's so beautiful."

I stood up. "Pardon?"

"You are hiking?"

"Um, yes."

"Then we go together. Come."

"Oh, you go ahead."

"You are waiting for someone else?"

"Well...no."

"So, come."

He made it sound simple, so I got up and followed him to the ticket kiosk. He greeted the attendant by name and they started talking in Hebrew and laughing.

He turned to me. "I told him we met in the desert. It's such a beautiful thing. Now he says you are my desert queen."

I burst out laughing. I wanted to say I was nobody's queen.

"Here." He reached for a bottle of water from behind the kiosk window. "You don't have enough. Take this."

I accepted it.

"You must drink all the water. Come, we'll go together."

I stammered, "Okay," and started to follow him down the trail.

The guy, whose name was Tal, rambled on about growing up in the desert, his years selling jewelry in Denmark, the best recipes for juicers and his job trucking in the north.

"You're religious, right?" he asked.

I nodded.

"You have kids?"

"No." The heat seared me, burning the back of my bare hands. I had trouble keeping up with Tal's pace. He kept stopping to let me catch up, but I never had a real chance to rest. I sucked at my water bottle continually.

"Then how can *Moshiach* come?" he asked.

"Pardon?" The heat made it hard to concentrate.

"How can the Messiah come if you're not having children?"

My hands became fists by my sides. "I just got religious."

"Then how is it your family lets you out alone?"

I licked my lips. "It's not like that."

"You know, the religious here, they don't have to serve in the army. They just study all day." His face twisted with resentment.

Would he ever stop talking? I wanted to stand and absorb the desert. Up close it was rocky and dirt brown. A cliff loomed to one side of the path, and on the other side, low bushes clung to a meager stream. My head felt strangely cloudy, as if I'd drunk too much wine. I stumbled a little on the path and then caught myself. I stopped to guzzle more water. Tal waited patiently. He didn't even look hot. My face throbbed and my skirt clung to the back of my legs. I sat down on a rock. "I think I'll rest awhile. You go on without me."

"Ah, but we're almost there. Besides, don't you know you aren't supposed to hike alone?"

"I don't feel so well." My head pounded and red spots flickered behind my eyes. I thought I might throw up.

"You are drinking your water?"

I held up one empty bottle.

"Headache?"

I nodded.

Tal hunkered down on the sand beside me and dug in his bag. "Probably you are dehydrated. Here, I have oral rehydration powder. It's for Egyptian babies but it works on American babes too."

"I'm Canadian," I mumbled.

Tal shrugged and poured a yellow powder into my water bottle. "Drink this."

I tipped my head back and drank the bitter liquid. I put my face in my lap and tried to block out the harsh light.

"Come. You'll feel better in the water."

I got up and shuffled down the path, head down, oblivious to everything except putting one foot in front of the other. My head ached and my legs were like jelly. At least I felt too crappy to think about Andrew or the trees.

When we arrived at the waterfall, I undid my hiking boots, threw off my hat and waded into the water, fully dressed. The water slipped over my head. Delicious coolness surrounded me. I could feel my skin drinking. Forget the desert, forget God and Allah. Truth was in water.

"I'm going to start a new religion—water worship," I told Tal.

"You feel better?"

"Yes, thank you."

"The desert is my home. I want everyone to feel welcome."

We crouched quietly in the water, side by side. I looked up at the cliffs, at the sun blasting into the tight hot canyon. The desert wasn't welcoming. It had sucked me dry. It wasn't the vast space I'd imagined.

Then a group of Israeli teens hurled themselves into the water, screeching and laughing. I stopped thinking about the desert and watched them splashing. They seemed so carefree.

I hiked back to the road with Tal. I still had a headache, but I no longer felt like throwing up. The bus wouldn't come for another hour so Tal invited me for a float in the Dead Sea.

The beach was only a couple of minutes walk down the highway from the bus stop. From the road I could see the pink and purple hills of Jordan on the other side of the water. I knew the Dead Sea was the lowest point on Earth and the high salt content of the water made it easy to float in. I didn't know it would feel like swimming in warm Italian salad dressing, or that the salt would make every pore on my recently shaved legs burn.

Tal laughed as I waded in and then barreled out to shower off at a tap on the beach. A group of men stared at me as I tried to rinse the salt off my stinging legs without lifting my skirt. Tal chuckled from the water. I silently swore under my breath and turned my back on them all. Some European women arrived in bathing suits and no one paid any more attention to me.

Thankfully the bus home was air-conditioned. I sank into my seat, happy to be out of the glare of the sun, away from Tal's appraising eyes. My head ached, my skin still stung from the salt, and my collarbone throbbed from sunburn where my shirt had slipped down. Israeli teens sat at the back and butchered Beatles' classics. Tal's voice rang in my head. *We meet in the desert. You are my desert queen.*

I sighed. I wanted to sit in my shower stall at home with the lights out, surrounded by the sound of the water pattering around me.

The bus slowed down. I looked up to see a man get off. He wore western clothes but carried a long knife at his waist. I couldn't see any towns or villages nearby, nor any of the squalid encampments of goats and shacks I'd seen on the way down. I craned my neck to watch the solitary figure head out into the desert hills. Where was he going? Did he live somewhere out there, beyond the roads?

I would never own the desert, I knew that now. You could only go in and survive, if you knew how. And the gorgeous views? Up close the desert was rocks and dust, not sand. Which was better? Standing and watching and not really knowing it, or walking and finding it different? Was there a third possibility? Could you go there and feel a connectedness? To love? To God? What if the two melded together? I wasn't sure, but I wanted to go back soon.

When I got home, Aviva was in our room, sprawled on her bed with her books and papers. She stared at me. "What happened to you?"

I ran my hands over my dirty T-shirt. The craft center went on a field trip? I had a new job volunteering in a sandbox? "Oh, I just walked a lot today," I said quietly, keeping my head down. I could feel her piercing gaze.

I knew Aviva hadn't believed me when I told her I'd been with Mrs. Shanowitz the night before when I'd really been with Andrew.

I turned my back so she wouldn't see my tattoo and pulled off my dirty T-shirt. I hoped she wouldn't ask any more questions. At the sink I splashed cool water over my red face.

"Are you sure you don't have heatstroke or something? Your face is so red."

"I did overdo it, but I'm feeling better now." I pulled off my skirt, shoes and socks, ignoring the small pile of sand falling around my feet. "I think I'll take a shower now." Aviva stared at me as I nudged the sand under my bed on my way out of the room.

ELEVEN

The air-conditioned lounge of the King David Hotel was deliciously cool. I sat directly under a vent and let the icy breeze blow directly on me. I closed my eyes and tried to focus on my surroundings: the well-dressed tourists, the expensive art on the walls, the neat waiters, even the Muzak in the background.

I held a stack of postcards in my lap, but I hadn't written a single word. *Dear Mom, I've met a boy. Dear Mom, They read the bible literally here. Dear Mom, They planted trees over people's villages.*

I kept thinking what Sheila would say if I told her about the *Nakba*. She'd be so outraged she'd get out her placards and start making signs to organize a protest. We'd stand in front of the Israeli embassy with Palestinian women. Sheila never just said, "That sucks."

She took action. I used to hate her protests and petitions. All her marching and knocking on doors embarrassed me.

And Don? He wrote songs about the world's problems instead.

Maybe I could just write a song. *Stolen trees bear sour fruit.* What rhymed with fruit? Root?

> *We try to set down new roots*
> *But stolen trees bear sour fruit.*

Too harsh? Maybe, but also true. Aviva would say they were stolen from us in the first place, that we were just taking them back. *Reclaimed trees bear sour fruit?* And who was the "we"? Was I really part of this?

I tapped my pen on my notebook and jotted more lyrics.

> *You say this is your ancestral land;*
> *We say these are our rocks, our sand.*
> *Does it matter who came first?*
> *Our prayers cannot quench our thirst.*

If I played the song, other people would know about the trees, and they could stand in front of bulldozers and oppose the government. I thought about driving a car like Don's station wagon miles and miles across North America to sing and then returning home, tired and depressed.

One of the reasons I became religious was to avoid the wandering, lonely lifestyle of a musician.

Two couples sat down at the next table. I heard a man say to one of the women, "How did you find the Dome?"

"It was amazing. Absolutely fascinating."

I turned to look at the tourists, two older couples in Tilley hats and expensive travel clothes. The backs of the men's necks were deeply lined by the sun.

One of the women said, "It just glints in the sun. I can't imagine what it's like when they're all there to pray. Stunning, I bet."

"We really thought it was the highlight of our trip. That and the Wailing Wall on the Sabbath."

The Dome. I had gotten used to its gleam, had become almost indifferent when I saw it on my runs. These tourists had walked where the *Ir Hakodesh* used to be, where the high priest had talked to God.

After Aviva said it wasn't a good idea to go, I'd put it out of my mind. Now I yearned for it. I wanted to walk on holy ground. It would take my mind off the trees. I got up from the table, paid for my drink and headed toward the Old City.

🌿

Half an hour later I clutched my backpack to my chest as I passed through the metal gate to the Temple Mount.

My pace slowed as I gazed up at the soaring Dome. A group of women in headscarves stared at me from under the graceful trees lining the walkway. I tried to keep my eyes forward. Did they think I was Jewish, or just some tourist? I passed a fountain surrounded by a wrought-iron enclosure and then stood in front of the stairs leading up to the Dome. I paused, trying to absorb the beautiful arches and intricate mosaic tiles before I entered. Inside was darker, cooler. My eyes adjusted and I could see the giant rock surrounded by a railing. Carved lattice windows shed intricate shadows on the floor. "*Kadosh, kadosh, kadosh,*" I whispered, involuntarily rising up on my toes. Holy, holy, holy. I closed my eyes and imagined Mohammed in a white robe sailing toward heaven, his arms reaching up like a lover in a Chagall painting. I felt my spirits lift, light and frothy, as if I too was soaring through the sky.

This spot with the rock. Did the ancient Jewish priests talk to God here? I felt a shiver run down my spine. I started to walk around the rock, humming a line from prayers. *Adonai melekh.* The Lord is King. If I could speak with God, what would I say? Would I pray for peace, or for the earth to go back to seed and start over?

I walked away as if in a dream, my feet moving through the plaza of the *Kotel* and the narrow alleys of the Jewish Quarter, until I stood in front of Andrew's hostel. I hadn't seen him since our afternoon in the park. I could hear Neil Young's "Helpless" coming from the roof.

I climbed the stairs to the roof deck and waved to Andrew. I pulled up a chair next to him and let the melody pour over me. It was as refreshing as entering the Ein Gedi oasis. I sang along, not caring how loud I sang. My smile was so big, I thought my face might break in half.

Andrew turned to me. "You look happy."

"I just went to the Dome of the Rock."

"Ah. Beautiful."

"Yes."

Then I saw Kyle walk up the stairs. When he winked at me, I pretended to study my sandals. He took a seat across the circle and started to play a bongo drum, poorly.

The song ended and the travelers chatted and drank beer. I sat watching the group, my gaze still on the Dome.

"We're building again tomorrow." Andrew's voice ripped me out of my reverie.

"What?"

"We're rebuilding a house, if you want to come. The bus leaves from Zion Square at ten o'clock." He had that serious look again. It made me want to grab him.

"Oh." My pulse throbbed like sonar at my temple. "I don't think so."

Andrew shrugged. "If you change your mind…"

Sheila would go, and drag ten friends with her. I shook my head. I'd stick with writing bad lyrics instead.

I found myself thinking about Andrew on the bus ride home. I liked how laid-back he was. I liked his slow wink, the casual way he held a guitar, his loping walk. Most of all, I was a sucker for a guy who listened like I was the only girl who existed. And Andrew actually cared about someone other than himself. I'd never met a guy willing to rebuild houses in the desert for other people.

I was still enveloped in a golden glow when Aviva came home that evening.

"How was your day?" Aviva put her backpack down on her chair and took a swig of water.

"It was great."

"Oh yeah? What were you up to?" She dug in her desk drawer and pulled out a bag of pretzels. "Want one?"

I shook my head and rolled over on my bed. "I can't tell you."

Aviva's eyes sparkled. "What?"

"It's a secret."

"C'mon. Now you have to tell."

I took a breath. "I know you said not to, but I went to the Dome of the Rock."

"Oh." Aviva's face fell.

I instantly regretted telling her. "I know Jews shouldn't go there, but I had to see it. And I'm glad I did. It's *so* beautiful."

Aviva's eyes darkened. "I hear they have a cloth stained with blood from the Hebron massacre right inside the mosque."

"I didn't see that. I just saw this beautiful rock and the mosaics."

Aviva crossed her arms against her chest and pressed her lips into a tight line.

"Just wait," I said. "I know you're mad, but listen…" I sat up and braced my hands on the table between our beds. "I thought, isn't it amazing both religions have the same holy place? I mean, think about it. There must be something really special about that particular piece of land. It's so full of *Hashem*. And *I* got to be there."

Aviva ripped her headband out of her hair. "Sometimes you are so naïve."

I ignored her. "I was thinking about Mohammed ascending to God from the rock, and how he was like one of the high priests talking to God. How cool is that? And I love the image of flying. It makes me think of the Chagall painting, you know the one where the lovers are flying. Do you think Chagall was thinking of Mohammed?"

"Chagall was a Jew," Aviva said tensely.

I flopped back on the bed. "It was a really amazing experience and you should go check it out."

Aviva stared at me. "How come you have all this time to wander around? Don't you go to class?"

"I dropped my *halacha* class."

"What? How come?"

"I was so sick of talking about what happens when the meat and cheese touch in the refrigerator."

"Actually it doesn't matter—"

"Who cares? Why aren't we talking about why God wants us to keep them separate? What's the context?"

"Sometimes you need to learn the details first."

I took a deep breath. "I'm more of a big-picture kind of a girl."

"I see."

Neither of us said anything. Our room felt very small, so I went to take a shower. When I came back, Aviva ignored me and kept reading. I lay on my bed, arms and legs tense, my mind racing. I wished I hadn't told her. My day was tarnished now with her negativity.

I took Andrew's bandanna out from under my pillow and lay with it over my face, taking small breaths, as if I was burying my face in Andrew's tanned neck, as if my hands were reaching around his chest. He understood how beautiful the Dome was. I rolled over onto my side and squinted at Aviva under the desk. How could she be so narrow-minded? I wanted her to read about the *Nakba*, to understand what was going on in the country she loved so much. But it wouldn't have the same meaning for her as it did for me. She believed in God the way the other B'nos Sarah girls did. If you read the bible literally, you could justify killing other people for the sake of a homeland: Israel was worth it.

And some Palestinians were willing to kill too. I felt a chill run down my spine. I was surrounded by God-driven violence. I glanced at the bible on my desk and shuddered. What a dangerous book.

I sat up, my head spinning. I wanted to rewind my thoughts. I became religious to bring love and peace into the world. But it seemed Judaism, at least in Israel, wasn't about the good of all humans, just the good of all Jews. Were all religions like that? It was like Dan said: you worried about your own people first. I'd wanted to be part of a community, but not at the expense of other people.

I wanted to pace around the room or go for a walk or, better yet, slam dance in a noisy bar. I leaped out of bed and rearranged the books on my desk. Aviva sighed and rolled over noisily. I glared at her and lay down again. I tried to calm my breathing. I could still bring love and peace into the world. I'd start tomorrow by helping rebuild that house. I clenched my fists. I wouldn't just stand aside. Andrew's bandanna was still on my pillow. I sniffed it again and let his image fill my head. I'd rebuild that house, with Andrew.

I dreamed about bulldozers all night. In the morning I drank too much coffee, and my hands shook when I tried to hold my book during morning prayers. Michelle was away writing her conversion exam and no one else would miss me all morning. I would be back in time to meet Aviva in the afternoon for choir practice.

When I got on the bus to go to the rebuilding site, I saw Andrew sitting at the back. I nodded to him and chose a seat near the front with two women from Hebrew University. They were wearing shorts and tank tops. I tried to tuck my running shoes under the seat so I wouldn't have to look at them next to my skirt. I was so sick of wearing ugly clothes.

The bus drove out of Jerusalem and into the brown hills for almost half an hour, until it stopped beside a bulldozer lifting a pile of rubble. We piled out of the bus and grouped around a man wearing a wide-brimmed hat and carrying a clipboard. He gave directions in Hebrew. I listened, not understanding. At the end he said in English, "If the police come, go back to the bus. That's all you need to know."

We lined up and passed rocks to clear a path to mark out a garden. I joined a group of women lifting lighter stones. Some of them were religious women in long skirts and long-sleeved shirts, their hair covered by hats or scarves. I wanted to reach out and ask them if it was really okay to be here. A woman passed me a stone and I passed it down the line. Andrew was somewhere else, out of sight. Under the stones lay squashed shrubbery. The sun burned my back and shoulders. The heat felt oven-like, claustrophobic. Sweat trickled across my stomach.

Exhaustion settled over me. We would never be finished. And wouldn't the army just come again? It would all be dust in the end.

When I straightened up, I expected to see Jerusalem over my shoulder, glinting. Instead a brown hill loomed, and then another. I kept working, moving. Stiffness built in my back and shoulders.

On a break I walked away from the group, over a slight hillock, out of view of the house. The desert was not the vast flat pancake I'd envisioned, nor was it enough space to empty out my mind. People and their memories, their longings and desires choked the land. I had wanted an empty place to drain the thoughts out of my buzzing brain. Here was no safe road.

I sat down in the sand and focused on the heat, my sweat, the yellow-brown of the dirt, trying to forget why we were there. I'd seen the Palestinian guy who owned the house. He looked like the Israelis, except maybe more weary. I couldn't imagine what it must be like to have your house knocked down. Tears pooled in my eyes, but I blinked them back, making my head ache. I needed to save my strength for my forearms and shoulders.

Rebuilding wasn't protest enough. We should have stood in front of the bulldozers to stop the house from getting knocked down.

The police did not come. The rocks became an orderly garden path. A woman planted some bushes in the new space and everyone clapped. Then we boarded the bus back to Jerusalem, to Zion Square. The city seemed loud and crowded after the quiet of the desert. Andrew approached while I was digging in my backpack for my wallet. "Hey," he said.

"Oh, hi."

"Do you have time for a drink?" His face was hidden behind his sunglasses.

I wanted to go home, take off my running shoes and clothes and get in the shower. The dust covering my skin made me feel itchy. "Neh, I don't think so." I avoided looking at him.

"Oh, well. Which way are you going?"

"Up to the bus stop."

"Me too." He fell in step beside me. I walked quickly. I didn't want anyone to see us together.

The street performers were out: a girl on a purple mat doing creepy pretzel contortions, the Russian with his pathetic marionettes, a man singing love songs. Tourists flocked to the souvenir shops. Israelis smoked cigarettes in the cafés and talked on cell phones.

Maybe for a moment we could sit and have a beer at the back of a café under a fan, even smoke a cigarette, and talk about music. I could lean close enough to smell him and he'd still make me feel like falling or flying, even with the layer of dust coating the light brown hairs on his arms.

I imagined bringing Andrew home to Sheila's tiny living room with the crazy Mexican masks decorating the walls, instruments crowding the shelves, our saggy sofa. We'd sit on the floor and I'd ask, What's your favorite recording? What was the first album you ever bought? What song did your mother sing you to sleep with? If your life was a song, what would it be now—tomorrow—last year?

And I'd tell him my mother sang me, "Goodnight, Sweetheart, Goodnight." I'd say I bought a Cindy Lauper album with my birthday money when I was eight, that I have a memory of my parents harmonizing "Michael, Row Your Boat Ashore."

At my funeral I want someone to sing "Summertime," and if I could sing like anyone, I'd be Joni Mitchell. Most of the time I want to stand up and wail out a gospel tune: "Sometimes I Feel Like a Motherless Child."

Surely I'd know more about him than the songs he could play: "Crazy" or a Beatles' medley.

We walked up the street. Andrew loped, leading with his head. It was an odd walk; I wanted to watch.

"So, how long are you staying?" he asked.

"I leave the end of August."

"And then?"

"Oh, back to Toronto. I start university in the fall. You?"

"Not sure yet." We went by the place he used to sing. "So, was rebuilding what you thought it would be?"

"Dirtier."

He laughed. "I'm trying to get a band together to go to this Palestinian school, do some more music workshops. You should come."

"I'm not sure I can lie that much."

Andrew gave me a quizzical look. "It has to be a secret?"

"Definitely."

My bus started to come down the street, the number 18. Traffic stuttered around the buses, stopping and starting, taxis honking. Young girls slipped by holding hands, their legs smooth. The sidewalk felt like a baking tray. I eyed the crowd thronging the bus shelter. I hesitated, not wanting to enter the swarm of hot bodies.

"Take the next one. Maybe it'll be less crowded." He gave me one of his sexy smiles, the kind that made me smile back. I sighed. The number 18 slowed to let a slew of passengers onto another bus.

"It'll be a while till the next one."

"So we'll go for a drink. I'll tell you about the band and the kids."

An old woman with a heaped-up shopping cart elbowed past me. At the back of the bus I noticed a man who looked like my Zeydi Abe, Sheila's dad. He had the same white bushy mustache and square glasses. I took a few steps back toward the bakery and watched my bus fill up.

Andrew leaned one hand against the dirty wall. "So why did you come build today?"

"I decided it was the right thing to do. *Gemilut hasadim*, an act of loving kindness."

Andrew laughed. "I like that—rebuilding Palestinian homes is a good deed."

"Every little bit helps bring the Messiah."

Andrew smirked.

"What?"

"You don't really—"

A deafening boom, like cannon fire, drowned out the rest of his sentence. A wave of heat burst over us, ripping through the air. I slammed my hands over my ears. A second explosion detonated, even louder, like planes roaring too close overhead. Andrew leaped over me, pulling me down behind the Plexiglas bus shelter. I heard a small thud; then my knees scraped across the pavement. The number 18 bus blasted into flames, pieces of metal ricocheting toward us, flames screeching, metal twisting upon itself into a red and gold prison. Andrew's body came down over me, like a human blanket.

The air filled with thick smoke. Ambulance sirens wailed. I saw metal barriers yanked over the falafel stand across the street. There was a taste in my mouth like burning meat.

"Get up!" Andrew wrenched my arm. I stood watching. Burn, baby, burn. My lungs filled with thick choking smoke, like a tarry barbecue. I let Andrew yank me down the street, stumbling on stones, scraping my knee on the pavement again. My retching throat made my feet move faster. Andrew's long legs sprinted down Ben Yehuda past the man with the marionettes to Zion Square. He kept my arm clenched tight in his fist.

I stopped to catch my breath.

"We gotta get out of here," Andrew yelled. Around us sirens wailed.

"Wait. Wait. Wait." I wanted to stay and understand what had happened. I was supposed to be on that bus. Now it was burning.

"Are you crazy? Are you crazy?" He tugged my hand. "What if there's another?"

I let Andrew yank me down Jaffa Road. He pulled me into a cab. In the taxi we sat panting. I still felt the heat on my skin. Burning, a bus burning.

"Yes," Andrew said.

Did I say that out loud? "Yes," I repeated. My voice sounded far away, across an ocean. There were noises in the distance. No, not in the distance.

"Am I yelling, am I yelling?"

"I'm not sure."

"Yes," the taxi driver said, "you are both yelling."

We stopped talking.

The taxi driver said, "Fucking terrorists," and spat on the curb. "Where to?"

I didn't remember the hostel stairs, but then I was in the kitchen, with a very large bottle of juice and an endless stack of saltines. People crammed the narrow room, all talking. Dirt lined the cracks of my hands, making them look like country road maps. Inside my shoes, sand gritted between my toes. I could wash my feet but I'd have to put my dirty socks back on. I wanted different shoes. Sandals with a heel, my red leather ones. I wiped a tear that kept forming in my left eye, and the lines on my hands became a trickling creek.

Andrew kept talking. "I told Mia to get on the next bus so we could get a drink because we were so thirsty. We were standing there and then this bus exploded, like a wall of flames. We ran."

Would he ever shut up? My head was still ringing. The scrape on my knee burned. My blood was smeared on Jerusalem stone. The juice bottle was not empty, but I could feel the liquid sloshing around inside me, like a swimming pool in my gut. Still, my teeth tasted like burning hair, like I had scorched the inside of my mouth.

"I want a shower," I announced. Andrew stopped talking and looked at me. My voice still sounded far away. I stood up and then sat down again. There was no shower there for me. I didn't have clean clothes or a towel. I rubbed my dirty hands against my temples and let my head fall down on my arms on the sticky plastic tablecloth. Marmalade or jam, a black smear, glued my forearm to the table.

Andrew started talking again. "I was looking at this girl, just this young girl, long stringy hair, backpack and

headphones, and she's not there anymore. She's not."
After a while I only saw his mouth moving.

Andrew's arms were caked with dust like my own. He
had a smear of ash on his forehead. A cut was bleeding
at his temple. Was that the small thud I had heard—his
head hitting the bus shelter?

The guy, my zeydi man. He was gone too. His family
was calling each other saying, *Are you all right, are you
all right?* And no one could get ahold of him. In a few
hours they'd start calling the hospitals. His body would
be unrecognizable. All over the city, people were fran-
tically calling each other. Who were the unlucky ones,
who were the ones not getting through?

I hadn't gone up in flames, but the zeydi had. He
was dead and I was still here, walking, talking, thinking.
I clasped my hands together to stop them shaking, but it
didn't help.

I checked my watch. It was four. When had the bomb
exploded? Aviva would wonder where I was. Shit, I was
supposed to play guitar for choir. I stood up abruptly,
knocking over my chair. "I have to go."

"Wait."

"I have to go."

"You look pale. You shouldn't just leave."

"I need to go."

Andrew grabbed my arms. We were alone in the
kitchen now. I took a deep breath.

"Are you sure you're okay?" Andrew's eyes looked wild. The cut on his head had started to bruise.

I was still shaking. Andrew kept holding me, his grip too tight. I could feel him trembling, could hear the sound of his labored breath. I paused, looking straight ahead at his chest. It was almost an embrace.

"My friends will think I died on that bus. I usually go home from volunteering then."

He let go of me. I teetered a moment.

I used the payphone in the lobby. The line was busy. My pulse quickened.

Andrew walked me to the gate for a taxi. "Do you have enough money?" A taxi would be expensive. I nodded. The cars rushing by seemed too fast, the sun too bright. I wanted to go back to the dingy hostel kitchen, to the safe four walls, to Andrew's repetitive voice. I wanted to sit very still. If only I could wash my feet there. I swayed a little as I got in the taxi.

Aviva was pacing our dorm lounge, the TV and the radio both blaring the news. Helicopters beat the air on their way to Hebrew University Hospital. Someone was crying on the couch. I clapped my hands over my ears.

"Oh my god, I thought you died." Aviva's arms locked around me. I held myself stiff. I wanted to collapse into her. I wanted to let words flow out and have Aviva listen. I couldn't get my muscles to stop tensing. A long walk.

I needed to keep moving until I lost that shaky feeling. I could walk to the end of the desert. Except it would be hot and boring and I was very tired. So tired. If I could relax my body, I would be able to return Aviva's hug, but she held Jerusalem stone.

"I looked for you at school. I called the place you volunteer. I called Michelle. I wanted to call hospitals." Aviva was sobbing, her thin shoulders shaking. She was wearing a *Torah Lives* T-shirt with sweat marks under the arms. "Where were you? Why are you so dirty?"

"I was building a house."

"What?" She ran her hands through her hair. "Why weren't you in class? No one has seen you all day."

"Michelle was away today. Her exam. I built a house instead," I said stupidly.

"What? I don't understand. I don't understand." Aviva started to pace. "I wait two hours, thinking you were on a bus that exploded, and you tell me you were building a house? Whose house?"

"I don't know. A demolished house. Palestinian. The army said it was in the wrong place."

"What?" Aviva's face turned red. Her hair stuck out several inches wider than usual, almost afro-like, as if she'd been running her hands endlessly through her curls. "You put yourself in danger for some Palestinian who doesn't like the rules? And then, oh great, his cousin comes and bombs you?" Her words cut into me like glass.

I thought, Who is this stranger?

I sat down on the floor and pulled off my sneakers and socks and fanned my toes. I walked to the sink in our room and hoisted a foot in and turned on the tap.

"What are you doing?"

"Washing."

I stuck my feet under the cold water. Aviva watched me rub soap into the brown caked dirt. The cold made my shaking stop. Now, sandals. Flat ones made of worn, suede-like velvet. I shoved my wet feet into the grooved toes and headed to the door.

"Wait."

"Later."

My stupid skirt flapped around my calves; my sandals slapped against my heels. People stared at me. I looked at my reflection in the side-view mirror of a parked car. Ash smudged my cheeks. My skirt was bloody from my skinned knee.

I walked around the neighborhood, looking at children playing in courtyards, at men carrying briefcases, until I was hungry and I needed to pee all that juice out of me.

Aviva was waiting for me in the hall in front of our room. I walked right by her into the bathroom. I stripped off my clothes and stood under the shower. I scrubbed my fingernails, brushed my teeth, shaved my legs. I washed my hair three times. When I came out I ate four slices of bread slathered in butter. I stood at the edge of the lounge, looking at the news on the TV. Aviva sat on the couch, watching with some other girls.

"That's my bus." I pointed to the carnage on the screen. Someone quickly turned the channel to a mindless yogurt commercial. I sat down on the couch and stared over the screen, trying to think of nothing. It could have been me on the bus. I could be dead.

⚜

In the morning I awoke with a sweaty start. My hair still smelled like smoke.

Aviva asked, "Are you going to go to class today?"

"I don't know."

"I'll stay here with you."

"You don't have to."

"It's okay. We could go somewhere quiet."

"No, thanks." I rubbed my eyes and shook my head. A cloud resided between my eyes. "I have a letter to write."

I went up to the roof with a stack of postcards and a pen.

Dear Don, I wrote.

A very large bomb went off and killed many people inside a bus I was supposed to take on the day I went to rebuild a Palestinian house. I'm thinking about this today as I sit on the roof which has a beautiful view of the Judean hills.

I wrote on a postcard of the *Kotel* with the Dome of the Rock in the background. Over the picture I wrote,

City of Peace, my ass. Then I crossed the whole thing out and blackened it into an ink blob, like a storm cloud over the Western Wall, because I didn't want Don to know how naïve I really was.

Aviva kept coming up with coffee, with water, with toast. I let it all go cold, ignoring her.

"Are you coming in now? Do you want me to microwave your coffee?"

I stared at the cup in my hand and gulped the whole thing cold. "Thank you, it was good."

"You should eat the toast."

I shrugged, ate it, went to our room and closed the door. I sat on the bed and waited to see if Aviva would follow me in. She didn't. I grabbed my journal and read the lines I'd already written. Then I added:

Stolen trees bear sour fruit;
We must find other ways to take root.

Buses burn, children cry,
City of Peace is a lie.

The lines sucked, but then I wrote:

These trees are like lovers,
Roots clasping deep.
Jerusalem, oh City of Peace,
Why must all your people weep?

Chorus:
What we all need is a new Jerusalem;
What we need is to start over again.

I could hear the melody under the words. I tried to
hear the guitar chords in my head, but they wouldn't
come. I closed my eyes and tried to sleep. I couldn't.
People were killing each other. We were demolishing
their houses, and they were bombing our buses. I wanted
to untangle who was right or wrong, but I didn't have
the whole story. I probably never would. I wished God
really was up in the sky, meting out justice, untwisting
right from wrong, like when you got in a fight with
your brother and you were both right and both wrong
and only a watching parent could figure out who really
started it all. If only God was like that.

TWELVE

I started to wake to the call to prayer again each morning. I had gotten used to it, had even slept through it, but now its plaintive wail set me on edge. I lay in bed, wondering about the people it was calling. I tried to imagine a Muslim girl thanking God for making the new day. I wondered what she thought of the trees, the burning bus, the bodies consumed by fire. How would she feel about using violence to defend her homeland?

I didn't leave our dorm for five days. I missed a week of school and the overnight trip to Massada. In the mornings I stayed in bed, pretending to sleep, until Aviva left for class. Then I'd wander around the dorm trying to shake the ringing sound of sirens out of my head, like I used to shake the water out of my ears at the lake. When I tried to write chords for my Jerusalem song, I saw train wrecks and volcanoes and the bus in flames, the metal twisted into a burning cage.

One morning Aviva woke me up before she left for classes. "The night hike you wanted to go on is tonight. Are you going to come?"

"Oh, I guess so."

"A bunch of us are going for dinner first, if you're up for it."

I shrugged. "Maybe."

"It would be good if you came. You could go to classes too."

I sighed. It all seemed so loud and overwhelming.

"Are your ears still bothering you?"

"They're fine now."

"Then you'll meet us for dinner?"

I nodded.

Aviva gave me the name of a restaurant off Ben Yehuda.

I got up, took a shower and got dressed in the red-and-white-checkered dress with the cinched waist I'd worn on the first day of school.

When I arrived at my Torah class, Michelle was sitting with a girl I didn't recognize. Michelle hugged me. "I heard what happened. Are you all right?"

I nodded. "How was your exam?"

"Look." She held out a necklace with a Jewish star dangling from it. "I'm Jewish now." She beamed.

"That's great. I'm really happy for you."

Michelle looked relaxed, even buoyant. She introduced me to the girl sitting at the table, Sofia, a Czech immigrant in the process of conversion. "You weren't here, and Sofia didn't have a *chevruta*…"

"That's fine." I waved a hand in the air. "We can all work together."

I sat down at the table with them, but I had trouble keeping up. Michelle's Hebrew had soared from all her studying.

During break Michelle and Sofia talked about a shower for Chani.

"Is that today?"

"Yes."

"Crap." I'd forgotten all about it.

"I was going to get a gift from both of us, but I didn't know when you were coming back."

"You could have called," I mumbled.

"What did you say?"

"Nothing."

On the way to Chani's shower, I stopped on King David Street to buy a present. The Judaica was too expensive. A stationery store had only candles and paper. I went into a lingerie store squished between shoe shops. I fingered a lace camisole. It felt cheap. I gawked at the price tag. I moved toward a table of panties. Did Orthodox girls wear thongs?

A clerk with dyed red hair asked, "Can I help you?"

"Everything is very expensive," I murmured, not looking up.

"It is for yourself?"

"No, a shower gift. Do you have any underwear? Maybe something a little sexy?"

The clerk pointed to a table. I sorted through checked boy-shorts, lacy thongs, shiny black briefs with cutout gauzy windows. A box hanging on the wall caught my eyes. Edible underwear. Ooh, fun. I picked the box off the wall without checking the size.

The shower was in an apartment building on a tree-lined street south of Rehavia. A giant crayon drawing of Chani's fiancé, Yosef, with the title *Pin the Kippah on the Rabbi* adorned the wall facing the door. I froze. Would we really play, or was it a joke? Girls hovered around a table of food. Chani sat on a couch by the table, opening gifts with some girls from Israeli dancing. I sat at the edge of the group, gnawing on carrot sticks. Chani received a wine carafe, candles and stationery sets. The girls passed the gifts around for everyone to admire and decorated Chani with the bows and ribbons from the wrapping. I eyed my gift, the jaunty little box sheathed in shiny red paper. Even the wrapping was loud. I bit my lip. I should have bought her a piece of pottery. The girls oohed and aahed over an embroidered *challah* cover Sarah Shapiro had made.

I whispered to Michelle, "What did you get her?"

"I gave my money to Nomi. She bought something from a bunch of us." Michelle pointed to a large box. "You?"

"Um, well, you'll see. I… "

Michelle's eyebrows lifted. I lifted mine too and tried to smile.

I thought about the panties again, their glossy indecent glow in the plastic wrapper. Oh my god, what if they weren't kosher? I never checked. I stood up abruptly and went back to the table and grabbed some chocolate-chip cookies. A silly nervous feeling came over me. I should leave, or grab the gift when no one was looking, claim a sudden rash, asthma, a migraine. How would a rabbi decide if they were kosher anyway? Would he visit the edible-undies factory and inspect the melting gelatin? I felt nauseous, yet also giddy.

I sat down with the group again and nibbled cookies with determination. Chani opened the large box from Nomi and the other girls and pulled out a hand-painted *challah* plate. "This is gorgeous." While everyone was still admiring the delicately painted porcelain, Chani opened my gift.

"Brace yourself for this one, baby," I whispered to Michelle. Chani unwrapped it and studied the photograph of the semi-clad couple on the box. She looked confused.

Michelle drew in her breath audibly. "You didn't."

"I did."

Chani's cheeks flushed. "Thanks, Mia. That looks like...like fun."

"You're welcome."

Michelle grabbed my hand and pushed me out to the narrow balcony.

"Do you really think we'll have to play Pin the Kippah on the Rabbi?" I asked.

"What were you thinking?"

"I don't know. I thought it would be...fun."

"Have you tried talking to someone, maybe one of the teachers at school? Or praying?"

"I pray all the time."

"Then you need to get help, professional help."

"I think I am beyond help. I think I'm seeing clearly for the first time."

Michelle stared at me like I was crazy. "I'm not sure we should be studying together anymore."

"Oh." I stopped. Of course she wouldn't want to be associated with the crazy girl. "Don't worry about it. I can find someone else." I waved a hand in the air. "I think I'll go now. Tell Chani bye for me."

"Mia, wait." Michelle looked concerned. "It's just—"

"No, it's okay. I understand."

I left Michelle standing on the balcony and started walking toward the Old City to see Andrew. I imagined telling him about the shower, rehearsing how I'd describe Chani's face when she opened the gift. He'd laugh and shake his head. I started to laugh, walking down the street. People looked my way, but I didn't care.

Andrew wasn't in his room or on the rooftop. In the empty kitchen I looked at the table where I'd sat in shock the week before. The room smelled of garlic. Dirty dishes sat in the sink, attracting ants. The room was silent except for the hum of the fridge. A dog barked somewhere in the distance.

Andrew had been with me in that horrible moment, when my ears burned and my skin hurt. After the noise subsided, just the two of us were left sitting together. He was with me when my head pounded and my ears rang. That crazy underwater feeling—only Andrew understood it.

I felt tired. I wanted to take a nap upstairs in Andrew's bed, to wrap myself in his Andrew-scented sheets. I could be safe there; it wouldn't matter if he was there, but if he was…I imagined us lying in the bed together and felt myself flush. I sat for a few more moments, and then I got up to go meet Aviva on Ben Yehuda for dinner.

As I was going down the steep tile stairs, I saw Andrew coming in from the street. Heat crept up my neck. I felt my pulse quicken.

"Hi." I pushed my sleeves up my arms and then tugged them down.

Andrew put down his backpack. "Hey, guitar girl. I was thinking about you."

"You were?" I held my breath.

"I was wondering if you were okay."

"I'm all right. You?"

"Sure, fine. As fine as I can be." Andrew leaned against the wall and took off his sunglasses. He had dark circles under his eyes. "I wasn't sure if you'd come by again."

Suddenly I wasn't sure I should have come. I was probably just some girl, some yeshiva girl, to him. I mean, that's what I was supposed to be. I took a deep breath. "I need some help with a song. I've got lyrics but no chords. I thought, maybe..."

Andrew smiled. "Sure, c'mon up."

"I can't stay now. I'm meeting friends for dinner. Another time." I held out a folded piece of paper. "Here are the lyrics. You can look at them if you have time."

He took them from me and I turned to go.

"Mia?"

"Yeah?"

"You sure you're all right?"

"Probably not, but I'll get by."

"Come by soon." He gave my shoulder a squeeze and I flinched. "Oh, sorry," he said. "Jeez, I'm such a loser."

I laughed. We stood looking at each other for a moment, my heart slamming inside my chest as I gazed into his clear blue eyes. I wanted him to squeeze my shoulder again, and oh, so much more. Finally I turned away.

Aviva was very quiet at dinner and silent next to me on the bus to the night hike. I figured she'd heard about

my shower gift. Michelle avoided me. I stared out the
window at the gritty brown and yellow hills. We passed
small villages littered with broken cars. Groves of banana
trees stood withered brown by the sun. Then it got too
dark to see, and the windows reflected my face back at
me. My eyes looked blank.

The bus stopped, and we descended into the darkness. When my eyes adjusted, I could make out a parking
lot and, in the distance, the low mounds of the Judean
hills. A full golden disk of moon shone high overhead.
Girls milled around the parking lot, excited and a little
nervous to be in the desert at night.

Our tour guide, a short stocky guy with dark curly
hair, rounded us up. He introduced himself, gave a brief
history of the area and led us into the moonlit desert
along a narrow path. The sand looked white, like a trop-
ical beach, not the hard yellow scrappy rock I'd seen
during the day. In the darkness I had to look carefully to
see where to place my feet. We climbed a gentle slope and
came to a flat clearing at the edge of a canyon. By then
my eyes had adjusted to the moonlight and the land felt
vast and wide. The night sky twinkled above us.

The B'nos Sarah girls huddled in small groups,
laughing and talking and looking around. I stood aside.
I wanted to drink in the sultry air. Then the tour guide
instructed us to find a spot to sit by ourselves. I lay down
near the edge of the cliff, away from the cheerful group,
my fingers digging in the sand.

Above me, stars spilled across the sky in unfamiliar constellations. I searched out groupings and gave them biblical names. A small cluster of stars was Leah's pot, another Jacob's ladder.

"This is the land of your foremothers and forefathers," the tour guide intoned. "Imagine, this is where Avraham walked with Sarah. This is the barren yet beautiful land where Isaac met Rebecca at the well. Moses guided the Jews from slavery in Egypt to freedom in *Eretz Yisrael*, the land of Israel. This is where our forefathers made their covenant with God."

The guide paused to let those images set in. Tingles ran up my spine; I was lying on the spot biblical heroes had walked.

The guide continued, "You've come from afar, but this is your homeland. This land here, it is yours. Take this time now and walk in the land and make it your own. Reclaim it as one of the Jewish people."

The guide stopped talking. All around me the B'nos Sarah girls sat, their eyes closed or focused down. Aviva rocked back and forth like she was praying. Michelle crouched down, stroking some stones. I let the sand sift through my fingers. Here Avraham made his covenant with God. Also, here Avraham thrust out Hagar because Sarah was jealous. Here was the land of banished Ishmael.

The desert at night was totally different from the other times I'd come, when it was so hot I could barely walk. I remembered the way the heat had closed in on me, the way it beat me down. Tonight the warm balmy air made the desert easy. Anyone could love a land like this. Anyone could claim it as theirs.

My land. The idea bubbled up my throat like a giggle, erupting out of my mouth. I tried to swallow it down. Aviva was pacing now, concentrating on the sand. Michelle sat with her shoulders hunched forward, looking straight ahead. Behind me were Chani and Sarah and Rebecca and the other B'nos Sarah girls, all communing with their ancestral earth.

I tried to imagine us as children of the bible, as inheritors of this landscape of rock and sand. Again I quelled an urge to snicker. At best we were the descendants of *shtetl* Europe, of snowy winters and dark forests, not this heat and light.

I couldn't keep the giggle down. I started to titter, softly at first and then louder. I imagined a bird's-eye view of us North American girls squatting in the sand, each proclaiming ownership of our own square foot. Then a choking belly laugh escaped me. I felt as carefree and reckless as I had been after Chani's shower. Eyes turned my way, staring at me. I saw Aviva gawking and Michelle's concerned look. Our land. I'd never heard anything so funny. I stumbled away from the group back to the bus.

The smell of pine needles on damp earth over steep rocks by a lake; the sound of frogs in the tall grass by a log; the sight of a heron skimming over the water. That was my land. Not these sandy hills.

The bus was quiet on the way home. I sat alone at the back, restless. Giddiness tinged with nerves kept me tapping my fingers on the window.

Once we were back in our room, Aviva turned to me. "What *the hell* were you doing?" I'd never heard her swear before. Her eyes were red, as if she had been crying, and the fluorescent lights made her skin look yellowish. Curls frizzed out of her ponytail.

I felt light-headed, almost dizzy. I stood with my weight on one foot, my hip jutted out. "Oh, it was just so fake. All that 'connect with the land' bullshit. Give me a break."

"I bet you think we should give it all away." Aviva clenched her hands.

"No, not all of it." I stalked across the room, letting my hips swing. I felt like going out, like dancing in a sweaty bar, waving a glow stick. "Why are you so angry?"

Aviva wrung her hands. "You ruined the moment. You were laughing when I was trying to pray at the most beautiful spot. It was…disrespectful."

"I'm sorry. I left as soon as I could."

"You know what your problem is? You just can't be part of a group." She sat down on the bed, shoulders hunched, her hands stuffed under her legs.

"Maybe. But all that land stuff, it's so narrow-minded. I can't accept this is only our land, especially North American Jews. How can we walk here and say, I'm a North American Jew and I'm entitled to land. You Palestinians, sorry." I gripped the rim of the sink.

"Israel is the only democracy in the Middle East."

I threw up my hands. "What good is a democracy if it doesn't recognize all its people?"

"You're judging by Western standards."

"What standards am I supposed to use?"

"Middle-Eastern ones." Aviva leaned forward and glared at me. "You think all those Arab countries treat Jews as nicely as we treat Palestinians? You think they don't want to push us into the sea? All the Arab countries kicked out their Jews after Israel was created. Jews who lived in Muslim countries can't go back to their homes. We have our own country, an army. We're supposed to stand aside and let terrorists do what they like?"

"No, of course not, but I don't see how the answer is more violence."

"That's reality, Mia."

"No, there must be a more peaceful way."

Aviva slapped her hands against her thighs. "You are so naïve. Look, this may sound grim, but this is what I think: there's just not enough land and water for everyone. We need to take care of our own first. Israel should be for Jews. Arabs should go somewhere else. There are winners and losers."

I clapped my hand over my mouth. "You couldn't care less whose land it really is because you've won, and the Palestinians have lost."

Aviva shrugged. "If you want to put it that way."

I stared at her. "You really think that."

"At least I'm honest."

"What's that supposed to mean?"

"Nothing."

"What's that supposed to mean?" My voice rose.

Aviva balled her hands into fists. She stood and walked over to me by the sink. "Let me ask you this. Why didn't you come back here after the bus blew up?"

"What are you talking about?"

"When the bomb exploded. You didn't come right home."

"No, not right away." I walked back toward my bed. "What are you getting at?" My cheeks grew hot.

"You were with someone."

"Yes, this guy I know. We were waiting for the bus together."

"A guy?"

"He's just this guy I know who plays music. He told me about the rebuilding, but we didn't go together. We were both waiting for the bus when the bomb exploded. Then he took me back to his hostel."

"And you never thought of calling?"

"Aviva, I could have been on that bus! I was in total shock." My voice got louder. "We sat around in this stunned silence and said things like, 'A bus burned, a bomb exploded. People died.'"

"And so you spent that time with some guy you know from playing guitar at his hostel."

"You're making it sound so indecent. This guy used to play guitar on Ben Yehuda near the bus stop. I gave him a *sandwich* because I thought he was hungry." I started talking faster, tugging on my knuckles behind my back. "We chatted and I played guitar at his hostel once. He told me about the book, about the *Nakba*, and when we talked about it again, he said I could help rebuild a house. I mean, I know this guy from lugging stones in the desert."

Aviva's mouth dissolved into a tight little line. "I saw you in the Old City today. I followed you to that hostel and I saw you with that guy. You were both laughing. I saw him touching you."

I felt like a balloon emptying of air. I struggled not to sway. "But it's not what you think."

Aviva glared at me. "The Torah says men and women—"

"I know what the Torah says."

"So why are you running around playing music and building houses with—"

"What do you care what I do anyway?" I thumped my fist on the desk.

Aviva paused. "People are starting to talk."

"Oh, I get it. You're worried about your reputation."

Aviva started to cry.

"That's it, isn't it?"

"I don't want it to be that way." Aviva settled back on her bed, hunched over her lap.

"But it is."

I let Aviva sob. Suddenly I felt badly for her. She didn't want to be the girl with the crazy roommate, just like Michelle didn't want to be the one with the nutty study partner. Around us the dorm was silent. I wondered if girls were listening from other rooms.

Aviva looked up at me. "He's so in love with you," she whispered.

"What?"

"Can't you see it? He's totally in love with you."

I stood up and walked across the room. "He's just a friend."

"Please, I saw the way he looked at you." She started sobbing again. "I've never had a guy look at me that way."

I paced back to my bed. I felt dizzy, so I sat down again and let my head rest in my hands.

Aviva wailed, "What are you going to do?"

"Shh." I needed to think. I sat for a few moments, my head swirling. I was hurting Aviva. I wasn't being fair to myself. I was deeply in love with Andrew.

Then I knew what I needed to do. I started filling my backpack with underwear, skirts, some fresh T-shirts. I worked quickly, adding my hairbrush and toothbrush, some deodorant and hair elastics. I added my journal, my Discman, Andrew's bandanna, some pens, my maps and my passport. I left my bible and notebooks on the desk. Aviva watched me, nervously gnawing on her fist. I took my sunhat, sunscreen and my water bottle. At the last moment I stuffed in my checked rockabilly dress.

"Where are you going?"

"To solve problems. You won't have to worry about your reputation anymore."

"You can't just walk out in the middle of the night." Aviva's voice was screechy.

"Why not?" I stood with my hands on my hips.

"It's not safe!"

I started to laugh. "Don't worry, I'm good at this kinda thing."

"The school will call your parents if you just take off."

"My parents?" I started to laugh. "My mother would probably love to know I was leaving." I could almost hear Sheila's sigh of relief a million miles away. "She's at some women's retreat, dancing naked and making pottery. And my dad..." I was starting to feel out of control. I took a deep breath and checked my desire to punch a wall or kick the door. "We haven't spoken in almost a year. You get the picture?" I swung my backpack over my shoulder. "See ya around."

"Mia, wait."

I didn't. I walked out of the dorm and headed to the road.

I took a taxi to the Old City. I could have run all the way just on adrenaline. At the hostel I took the stairs to Andrew's room two at a time, knocked on the door and waited. No one answered. He wasn't on the rooftop with the other hostellers or in the kitchen. I ignored the sick feeling starting to twist in my stomach. Then a girl told me Andrew was house-sitting near the café we'd eaten at on Emek Refaim. A bunch of people had gone over earlier to hang out. She gave me the address.

My stomach tightened even more as I walked through the dark streets. I wasn't sure exactly where I was going. I didn't know Jerusalem at night. What if Andrew wasn't there either? What if he said, "What the hell are you doing here?" I circled the Jerusalem Theater twice, squinting at my map in the lamplight. I tugged on the ends of the bandanna covering my hair.

When I finally found the house, it was after 11:00 PM. I peered through the fence and bushes to see if there was a light on. I couldn't tell. I sat on the sidewalk a minute and took a few deep breaths. He could be busy. He could be out. Then I thought about the way he had looked at me that afternoon. I got up, straightened my skirt and rang the bell.

Andrew opened the door. His hair was uncombed. He rubbed his eyes sleepily. "Hey, what are you doing here?" He looked surprised to see me.

"Did I wake you?"

"No, I was just reading. Aren't you supposed to be in your dorm?"

"You mean locked up?"

"They don't really do that, do they?"

THE BOOK OF TREES

"No, I was just kidding."

"So?" He leaned against the door jamb. His eyes appraised me.

"I was wondering if we could look at those lyrics I gave you."

He furrowed his brow. "Now?"

I started to panic. "If it's too late, I'll come another time."

Andrew hesitated, squinting at me. "No, now is good. C'mon in."

I stepped inside a narrow hallway and followed him into a living room with low couches and an elaborately carved octagonal coffee table. He sat on a couch in his jeans and T-shirt, his bare feet tucked under him, and reached for his guitar. He started to tune it.

I perched on the edge of a chair across from him and focused on trying to find my journal.

Andrew tuned the A string. "So, you get in trouble?"

I kept my eyes on my backpack. "My roommate saw me at your hostel."

"We only talked a moment." Andrew looked up.

"It was enough. She knows—" I stopped. My face burned. Andrew looked back down at the strings. "Here." I reached for the guitar. He handed it over and I quickly finished tuning it. "I never played for you like I said I would."

He gestured for me to go ahead.

I slid over the armrest of the chair and curled into the cushions. Then I took a deep breath. I tried to clear my head of the sound of Aviva sobbing, of her angry words, of the sensation of fleeing. I tried to brush away the nerves clawing at my stomach, focusing instead on the image of Andrew waiting patiently for me to start. I played a few scales and some random chords; then I closed my eyes. I played the first songs I ever learned on guitar: "Country Roads," "Scarborough Fair" and "Brown-Eyed Girl." Then I played Fred Eaglesmith's "Wilder Than Her" and Don's song "Journey," about his father coming from Ireland. I played "Summertime" for Sheila, slow at first, thinking of cotton fields and a small black girl dreaming of angels, and then I played a jazzy version.

Andrew lay back against the cushions, eyes closed, mouth relaxed, sexy forearms crossed over his chest. He opened one eye and grinned at the second version of "Summertime."

"That's it?" he said.

"No, there's more." I played the mournful opening chords to Don's tree song, "Weeping Willow."

You said you could always come home,
But it'd never be the same.
Oh, Momma, I'm getting old as you,
But I fear I'll never be as wise.

Call off the bulldozers,
Call off our western ways.
This progress, I'll have none of it,
'Cause I lost my weeping willow, where I used to sit.

When I finished I leaned back, the guitar across my lap.

"It's a beautiful song."

"Thanks."

"It makes me think of the trees in Liberty Bell Park."

"I haven't been back."

"I ruined it for you," Andrew said softly.

"Yes."

"I've ruined lots for you."

I shrugged.

Andrew sat up on the couch and drew his knees into his chest. "C'mere." He patted the couch beside him.

I hesitated, and then I stood up. The space between the chair and the couch seemed huge. I took three steps and settled beside him. His arm lay across the back of the sofa.

"Mia Quinn." His fingers were so close to my shoulder he could almost touch me. "What are you doing here?"

"I can't be at my dorm anymore."

"Why not?"

"I can't—I can't lie anymore."

Andrew bit the corner of his lip and tapped his fingers on the couch. "Who are you lying to?"

"My roommate." I swallowed. "Myself." I whispered. "You."

Neither of us said anything for a long moment. I kept my eyes on Andrew.

"Can I ask you something?" he said. The lamp cast shadows across his face.

I felt my stomach tighten. "Okay."

He leaned back against the armrest, a playful smile across his lips. His fingers danced on the sofa. "How come you've always got your hair covered up?"

My hands flew to my bandanna. "It's neater. And cooler."

"Oh." Andrew closed one eye, looking at me with the other. "I saw you with your hair down once."

I blushed. Moments seemed to tick by. I didn't move.

Andrew leaned in closer to me. I could feel the heat of his body near mine, smell the sweet scent of his skin. My heart was racing. If I leaned just a little bit, I could brush my lips against his neck.

"Will you show me your hair?" he whispered.

I nodded, then hesitated. My hands hovered near my head. Then I leaned back and untied the knot in the bandanna and let it fall to my lap. My hair was in two tightly coiled French braids. I reached up to release the pins, and my braids fell down my back, like two snaky ropes. Then I pulled out the elastics and shook my head, running my hands over my sore scalp. My hair fell around my face.

My heart pounded as Andrew looked at me. His eyes followed the hair falling over my neck and down to my shoulders. My arm hairs stood at attention.

He reached out to touch me. "Can I?"

I nodded.

"Are you sure?"

"Yes."

I held myself still. Andrew slowly smoothed my hair over my head and then down my shoulder. Then he lightly brushed it away from my neck, sending shivers down my spine. He moved his hands through my hair, grasping my scalp, bringing my face toward him. Our lips touched and I was drowning in his intoxicating scent.

THIRTEEN

I woke up the next morning to light spilling across my face. A breeze knocked the window blind back and forth across the sill. I covered my eyes and rolled over, snuggling my face into Andrew's shoulder as if I'd done it a million times. Andrew pulled me toward him. I nuzzled his skin the way I'd wanted to since the first time I smelled him. I drew my fingers slowly down the smooth skin of his back. My lips traced small kisses from his ear down to his shoulder and then across his chest, briefly rasping a nipple with my teeth. I heard him sigh. I wanted to know the expanse of his skin, the breadth of his muscle. My nose pushed up under his arm and around the back of his neck. Andrew let me explore, his breath quickening. Our legs intertwined and his warm arms snaked around my waist until we were tangled together.

"I'm so glad you came here last night," he whispered.

"Me too." I gave him a kiss.

We made love slowly, eyes closed in sleepiness, just two bodies moving together, pressing, with none of the uncertainty or speed of the night before. As he slowly came inside of me, I resisted the urge to press him deeper, faster into me, letting him tease me until my breath came too fast, too loud, and I became just limbs, pounding blood and sweaty hair. Andrew collapsed on top of me, his weight pushing me into the mattress. We drifted back to sleep, the blind still wafting across the open window.

When I woke again, I was alone. I stretched lazily and buried my head in the sheets to inhale Andrew's smell and my own mingled together. A Gauguin poster hung above the mattress on the thick plaster wall beside the open window. Wooden beams crossed the ceiling. I padded down the cool tile stairs to the living room and into a narrow kitchen. "Andrew?" A note on the table read, *Gone for groceries. Juice in fridge,* and then a scrawled *A.* I wrapped my arms around myself and squeezed tight. A huge smile spread across my face and I did a small jig around the kitchen. I felt like I was in a goofy Broadway musical.

Then the doorbell rang. I was only wearing a skirt and tank top, so I grabbed Andrew's shirt from where I'd pulled it off him the previous night. Through the window I saw Kyle tapping his toes in his sport sandals. Shit. I slammed myself against the wall, but he had already seen me.

"Mia?"

I opened the door. "Hi."

"Hey, what are you doing here?" His eyes traveled from my mussed hair to the too-big T-shirt exposing my bare arms.

I stuck my arms behind my back. "Andrew should be back any minute."

"Oh." He smiled his cocky smile. I could feel my face burning. "I left my backpack here last night. I'll just pop in and get it, if that's okay." He started moving into the house. I stepped out of his way. Kyle disappeared into the living room and came back with the bag a moment later.

"You can stay until Andrew comes back."

"No, that's okay."

"All right, see ya."

"Bye."

I closed the door. Shit shit shit. Of all people.

I watched Kyle walk down the path. Just as he opened the gate, Andrew came up with grocery bags. I opened the door a crack to watch them.

"Dude." Kyle slapped Andrew on the back. "I knew she wanted you."

My face burned again. I jammed my curled toes against the stone floor. I couldn't make out Andrew's expression behind his sunglasses.

Then I heard Kyle say, "You owe me. Pay up."

I sucked in my breath, freezing against the wall. I pushed so hard on my toes they cracked against the tile.

"That's twenty bucks. I won." Kyle slapped Andrew on the back again.

Andrew waved him away. "I'll call you in a couple of days." Then he came in and saw me.

"Mia?"

I backed away.

"Hey, wait."

My feet slapped across the stone floor to the kitchen.

"It's not what you think."

I stopped by the kitchen sink. "You had a bet I'd come here?"

"It's not like that. It's just Kyle talking." He waved a hand in the air.

"You had a bet?" Tears rolled down my cheeks.

"No, I never did." My eyes narrowed to slits. Andrew took off his sunglasses. "Please, look. Kyle said something stupid like, 'That girl is so hot, and she wants you.' He said, 'I bet she leaves whatever nunnery she's in and comes to find you.' And I said, 'No, she's not that kind of girl.' And he said, 'You wait and see. I bet you twenty bucks she'll come.' And I said, 'I really don't think so.' I never agreed to the bet. I don't even hang out with him much."

"He left his bag here."

"A bunch of people came over last night."

My eyes were swollen and I was sobbing now. I turned away from Andrew and leaned against the fridge. I'd left everything—school, Aviva—for this guy. What if he turned out to be a jerk? My heart creaked in my chest. What if he wasn't in love with me? I'd become religious to avoid this kind of shit.

Andrew pulled me toward him until we were standing close, almost touching. "It doesn't matter what he thinks." He reached out to chuck me under the chin. I pulled away.

What now? What now? My head felt fuzzy and I wasn't sure if it was from lack of sleep or if I was in shock. I felt dizzy. I slumped to the side, leaning on the counter. I was unfurling, like a fern in the woods near Don's cottage, but instead of turning my edges up to the dappled light, I was collapsing. A pain throbbed in my chest and my breath came short. I pressed my knees tightly together, my shoulders hunched.

"I think…I think I need to lie down."

"Please, don't run away." Andrew's hands grasped my shoulders.

"I'm so confused."

Andrew tipped my face up so that I was looking at him.

THE BOOK OF TREES

"I'm supposed to be at yeshiva, not here," I whispered. "And your friends think I'm trash. I need"—my voice wavered—"I need a space. To lie down." My nose started to run and I turned my head. Andrew let me walk away.

I climbed the cool tile stairs back to the second floor and lay down on the mattress in the bare room with the Gauguin poster. My limbs felt heavy, as if they were made of bags of sand or water.

I wanted to be a reborn Jew so I could be new, so sex could be sacred, so I would only ever be with someone who truly loved me. And here I was, fucked up all over again. I fell asleep crying.

Someone was calling my name. I woke up slowly, as if emerging from the bottom of the sea. Andrew was saying, "Mia?" His hand stroked my shoulder. I sat up with a start. Sweat had crept around my hairline, and my mouth felt gluey.

"I'm sorry. I didn't mean to scare you."

I squinted into the light and rubbed my eyes. "It's okay."

I sat up next to Andrew and leaned against the wall. I had that fuggy feeling—congested yet drained—you get from crying yourself to sleep. I took a few deep breaths and looked at the cool walls, the fan whirring overhead. Andrew waited patiently for me to wake up.

"You okay now?"

I nodded.

"Are you hungry?"

"Um, I think so."

"I made breakfast."

I sat up and pushed my hair out of my face. "How do you know what I like?"

"I made lots of stuff. You'll like something. Come."

I sat there looking at him, at his lithe arms, the way he cocked his head to the side and squinted at me a little. A shiver ran through me. I wanted to memorize the arch of his brow, the angle of his cheekbones, the way his stubble darkened his jaw line. He looked so cute with his hair all mussed up and his eyes squinting into the light. I wanted to pull him back into bed with me. He couldn't have made that bet. Not Andrew, who helped rebuild houses. And if I didn't believe him, where would I be?

He stroked my cheek for a moment. "Come." He held out his hand and pulled me up. Only yesterday we'd never even kissed. I reached for my bandanna to wrap around my hair, but Andrew pulled it out of my hands. I let it fall to the floor.

On a tray on the living-room coffee table, Andrew had set out toast, scrambled eggs, hummus, cheese and an Israeli salad of cucumbers, tomatoes and peppers.

"Do you drink coffee?"

"Yes."

I sat quietly on a cushion. Andrew kept busy dishing out food for me, getting coffee from the kitchen. I thought he suddenly looked shy, a little eager to please. I kept my eyes on my plate. I was ravenous.

"So, whose house is this?"

"My manager at the museum. He and his family are away in Europe for a couple of weeks."

We ate in silence, avoiding each other's eyes. The eggs were delicious, the toast a little burnt.

When we were finished, Andrew held my hand across the table. I could tell he was studying my face. When he traced my cheek with his finger I leaned into his palm and sighed.

"What's the matter?"

"People will be worried about me at school."

"There's a phone in the kitchen."

"I'm not sure what to say... "

"Say you're not coming back."

I paused, staring at him, trying to read his face. I could feel my pulse throbbing in my temples. He looked calmly back at me. "You don't want me to go?" I asked.

"Do I have to say it?"

I tugged on the ends of my hair. "Yes."

"Don't leave."

I looked at his eyes, trying to drink in what I heard. Tears filled my eyes.

"Don't go anywhere. Why are you crying?"

"I'm not sure who I am anymore. I mean, I'm supposed to be this religious girl, but look at me."

Andrew leaned back in his chair. "What do you want?"

"To stay here with you. And play guitar."

"We could write some songs."

"Okay, but—"

"But what?"

"You don't understand. I'm supposed to be waiting for my *b'shert*, my one true love. And when I find him, I'm supposed to get to know him, then get married." It was too ludicrous to say aloud. "I don't even know you."

Andrew laughed. "I guess you're sort of off track."

"It's not funny."

But it was, and I was laughing and crying at the same time. I shook my head in my hands.

Andrew took my hand and laid it on his. "Let's go away together for a while. You can think about your school while we're gone."

"Where would we go?"

"Somewhere we don't know anyone, where we can swim and just hang out and get to know each other. You can think things through."

And have sex—lots and lots of it. As we were talking, my eyes stroked the curve of his shoulder. I wanted to plant kisses in the hollow of his collarbone. What would it be like to lie on his back and let him take all my weight?

"Yes, let's go away. Somewhere far."

"Dahab?"

"Sure. Where's that?"

"Egypt. The Sinai peninsula. There's diving and beer and pot. You probably aren't into that…"

My mouth started to water at the thought of a joint. "I might be." Yes, that's what I wanted: drug-induced oblivion, not to have to think.

We kissed across the table. Andrew's hands moved across my skull, clasping my hair. I could taste the garlic from the hummus on his lips. Andrew leaned back against the cushion. "So what do you want to know about me?"

"Um, what do you sing in the shower?"

"'The Night They Drove Old Dixie Down.'"

"Really?"

"Sometimes. Other times it's Nirvana. How about you?"

"I don't sing in the shower."

"Then why did you ask me?" Andrew folded his arms across his chest.

"I don't know. Let me try again. Favorite ice-cream flavor?"

"Rocky Road."

"Okay. Chinese or Indian?"

"Chinese. You?"

"Sushi." I sat smiling across the table.

"C'mon, hit me again." Andrew gestured like a boxer.

I cocked my head to the side. "Do you have a dad?"

Andrew sat up a little straighter. "I did. A long time ago."

"What happened?"

He exhaled a long breath. "He left my mom and me, and then he died a few years later in a car accident."

"Oh."

"Yeah."

We were both quiet for a moment.

"How about you?" Andrew asked.

"I've got a dad. He's…elsewhere."

"Is he coming back?"

"Not sure."

"You care?"

I nodded and felt tears bulging behind my eyes. "More than I should."

"No such thing."

"You think?"

"Otherwise you'd be dead inside."

"Uh-huh."

"Let me ask you one."

"Okay." I felt a little nervous.

"Best meal."

"Oh, easy. Scrambled eggs, toast, a little burnt is okay, Israeli salad with lots of tomatoes, and coffee. Strong and sweet."

Andrew batted me with a magazine.

We went outside to a small backyard garden shaded by high walls, an orange tree and jasmine. I could hide here forever, I thought. We settled into wicker chairs and I sang the chorus from my New Jerusalem song. We worked out a melody for the verses. As I sang, *trees like lovers, roots clasping deep*, I imagined myself singing in a smoky bar wearing jeans, cowboy boots and a skinny tank top. A shiver ran down my spine and I couldn't tell if it was attraction or revulsion or a bit of both.

We stayed in the house for the next couple of days drinking beer and playing old Beatles' songs, Simon and Garfunkel and U2. I played Andrew rockabilly songs from the Neon DayGlos and listened to him sing Elton John songs from his childhood. I played until my fingers blistered, until I was hoarse.

Andrew left to get groceries and to book our bus tickets to Sinai. I went for a run in the unfamiliar neighborhood and did sit-ups and push-ups on the cold stone floor. One afternoon Andrew took me to the school where he'd been volunteering in East Jerusalem. The boys jumped on him and the girls smiled shyly. They all sang a song about peace they'd written with Andrew. Then he taught them the chorus to my New Jerusalem song. Andrew recorded it on a mini tape recorder. We played the scratchy recording over and over again in bed that night, listening to the children's voices singing my words. I held my breath each time.

The next day I went back to B'nos Sarah to get some of my stuff. It was midmorning and I thought everyone would be in class, except—shit—it was Friday and I'd forgotten about Shabbos. The dorm hummed with girls getting ready for the weekend. I hesitated at the entrance, surveying the girls chatting and lugging backpacks through the lounge. Already I felt different from the girls in their denim skirts and pastel T-shirts.

I ducked my head and scurried to my room. Aviva wasn't there and some of her makeup was gone from the shelf. She'd probably gone for Shabbos to Dan and Leah's.

Our room looked like I'd never lived there. Only some books and a tube of hand cream lay on my side. I grabbed the crossword puzzle from a newspaper on the desk and lay down on my bed. *An Indian nanny: ayah. Three letters for brown-eyed girl: Van.* I lay listening to the sounds of girls talking in the lounge outside my door. Somewhere girls were singing, *"Lo yisa goy el goy cherev."* Nation shall not lift up sword against nation. I was alone again. No, I had Andrew. It wasn't the same. I wanted to be part of a choir, not a soloist. Could I stay for Shabbos dinner with the other girls and then sneak back to Andrew's bed? No, it didn't work that way. If I wanted to be like Aviva, then I couldn't be with Andrew. I sighed. I wasn't going to have Shabbos with a family that night. Would I ever again?

On my side of the desk was a postcard from Don with a picture of a canoe bobbing on a lake. It must have arrived while I was with Andrew. I grabbed it off the desk.

Dear Mia,
Long weekend at the cottage?
Love Dad

I thought about sitting on the saggy front porch of the cottage and looking down at the water rippling beyond the trees. Maybe I could just move my flight up and go home right now. I imagined getting in Sheila's car and driving up north and doing nothing but sitting on the dock with my legs in the cool water.

I left a note for Aviva saying I was going away for a week and asking her to let the school know I was fine.

When I got back to Andrew's I decided to make Shabbos dinner: salad, chicken and rice. Andrew tidied the living room and made brownies. It almost felt like Shabbos—the house was clean, there was plenty of food and we had showered for dinner—except there was just the two of us, and we were strangely quiet. As I started to serve the food, Andrew asked, "Aren't you supposed to bless the bread or something?"

I'd already lit the candles in the kitchen alone. I didn't have a *challah* and we were drinking beer, not wine. I shook my head. Andrew studied my face. I bit my lip and then started eating. We didn't talk much during dinner.

I wished we'd gone to Tel Aviv instead of acting out this charade. We were done eating before sundown, when Shabbos actually started. After we cleaned up, I sat on the low couch in the living room, aware of the silence around me. It didn't feel like Shabbos quiet.

"Let's go for a walk," Andrew suggested.

Outside I could feel the expectant quality of the day of rest: seeing friends, dinner with family. The streets were almost empty of moving cars. Families walked to *shul*, dressed in their clean, fancy Shabbos clothes. I clung to Andrew's hand and tried to focus on the trees lining the streets. We started walking toward the Old City. I let Andrew lead me through Jaffa Gate and then through the narrow city streets toward the *Kotel*. The sky had turned a beautiful mix of blue and pink. Huge floodlights lit the packed plaza below.

As we walked down the stairs, a circle of yeshiva boys burst into a singing and stamping dance, their arms wrapped tightly around each other. A group of girls formed a more sedate circle, singing a song to welcome in Shabbos. I thought I saw Chani and Rifka dance by. My heart ached to dance and sing with them. In only forty years the Jews had established such a beautiful country. Why couldn't I enjoy the mix of ancient and modern history and feel proud to be a Jew? Why couldn't I turn off my brain for five minutes and do a *horah* with everyone else?

Andrew nudged me. "Why don't you join them?"

I shook my head. I couldn't. Not when I knew what was going on in this country. I slumped down on a bench. I wasn't one of the B'nos Sarah girls. I never would be.

Off to the side a group of women started singing *Lecha Dodi*, a song to welcome the Shabbos queen. I quietly joined them. I didn't think about the meaning of the words, just let my heart fill with all my wishes and hopes: for a feeling of peace, for guidance for my divided heart. I wanted to be back at yeshiva praising God, with Andrew harmonizing Beatles' songs, and also with my parents at the cottage, roasting un-kosher marshmallows over a campfire.

After the prayers I found Andrew patiently waiting for me on the bench. He raised one expectant eyebrow at me, as if to say, how was it?

I sighed and took his hand. "Let's just go." And we started the long walk home.

When we got back to the house, all the lights were out and the garden was dark except for faint shadows from the waning moon. We stood on the front walkway between the thick bushes. Andrew reached for the key.

I grabbed his hand. "Let's just stand here a moment." I leaned into him and he leaned back. I had a sudden urge to push him hard, or smack my knuckles into the trunk of a tree. I gave him a shove with my palm, more forceful than playful.

Andrew stumbled backward. "What are you doing?" He gave me a slow, concerned smile.

"Push me back."

"What are you talking about?"

"Push me back."

"I don't want to hurt you."

I wanted him to shove me out of my funk. I came up close to him. "Just push me."

He nudged me with his shoulder, more a tickle. "Is this a game?"

"Yes."

"Should I let you win?"

"No."

Andrew took a step toward me and pushed against my shoulders with both hands, not forcefully, but with enough effort to send me backward. He grabbed my hand before I landed in the bushes. "Don't do that again," he said as he pulled me to him.

Andrew unlocked the door and held out his hand to stop me from entering the house. "Wait, I'll find the switch."

I slipped around him, blocking the light switch. "Don't bother."

"You'll trip."

I slid my palms up his arms and left a rough wet kiss on his chin. He kissed me back, leaning me up against the wall. Then I slipped out of his arms.

"Hey, where you going?"

"I'm right over here."

"Where?"

I hovered near the couch.

My eyes adjusted to the light and I could see the outline of Andrew across the room. He moved toward me and stumbled on the carpet. "Shit."

"Are you okay?" I started to giggle.

I heard him swear again under his breath. I darted into the kitchen.

"Mia?"

I waited silently in the dark, my pulse threatening to explode in my temples. I put my hand over my chest and took a few deep breaths. Finally I popped my head through the living-room door frame. "Hey, where are you?"

Hands reached out and grabbed me. I screamed as Andrew pinned me onto the couch. "Game over," he panted in my ear.

I squirmed with delight.

Two days later we got on the bus to Dahab. Except for a group of religious American girls, foreign backpackers filled most of the seats. I breathed a sigh of relief; no one on the bus was from B'nos Sarah. I gripped Andrew's hand as we left Jerusalem. I felt like I was abandoning B'nos Sarah, and at the last minute someone from school would order me back to class. I stared out the window, exhausted from the week of being bombarded by emotions. If only I could be two people, I'd be complete. I concentrated on slowing my breath and relaxing my body, keeping my eyes on the landscape.

I was almost asleep when I noticed the rolling Judean hills had changed to the flat pancake of the desert. I drew in my breath sharply and sat upright in my seat. The land extended endlessly to the horizon, the sky above huge and almost white in its brightness. I put my face up close to the window. If I could stand in all that space, I could…I wasn't sure what I wanted anymore.

I grabbed Andrew's arm. "I need to get off the bus."

Andrew turned to look at me. "Now?"

"Yes, now. Just for a few minutes. This is the desert I've been looking for." I knew it sounded weird, but I didn't care.

"Mia, you can't just get off here."

"But this is what I need." I stood up to get my backpack. The bus lurched, and I steadied myself with the seat.

Andrew grabbed my hand. "What are you talking about?"

"I—I have this thing for the desert."

"Please, sit down. I promise you, where we're going there will be endless sand."

"Not just the sea?"

Andrew nodded. I hesitated, still standing.

"If you need to, you can take a taxi out to the desert and do whatever you need to do," he said.

I looked out at the vista passing by, swaying with the bus. I could always come here on my way back if the desert wasn't the same in Sinai. I sat down.

Four and a half hours later we were at the border, crossing from Eilat to Taba, Egypt. After the air-conditioned bus, the heat felt suffocating. I let Andrew guide me through customs, following his sweaty back through the lineups. The heat dulled me, making my blood feel slow and viscous. In Taba we caught another hotter, more rickety bus to Dahab. Hot dry air blew in through the open windows, combining with the loud Arabic pop music blaring through the speakers. I sat still, letting the heat and noise rush over me. The religious girls were gone, probably to visit Mount Sinai.

In Dahab we got off the bus and trekked down a street of hostels and guest houses along the beach. I let Andrew choose a guest house with a view of the water and followed him up a steep set of tile stairs to our room. I lay on the bed and tried to let my limbs relax into the saggy mattress. Andrew opened the sliding patio doors, tried out the hammocks on the balcony and tested the water in the bathroom. Then he lay down on the bed next to me. He wrapped his arms around my waist. I kept tensing my leg muscles and shifting from side to side. I thought here I would be just Mia, whoever that was, a girl on vacation with a guy she was in love with. But my backpack was still full of long skirts and modest T-shirts, and I was in a foreign country with a guy I didn't know very well.

I wasn't going to be eighteen for another three months, and I hadn't even told my mother where I was.

"I'm going to go out for a bit," Andrew said. I nodded and watched him put on his sandals. I dozed, dreaming about the desert I'd seen from the bus, the desert where I imagined you could stand and be anyone or no one, as if you were hollow.

Andrew came back a half hour later with a six-pack of beer and a bag of pot. I watched as he rolled us a joint. The first hit burned my nostrils as I exhaled, but the second sent a wave of calm through me. I leaned back on the pillows and watched the yellow fuzz of the dimming light coming through the slats on the balcony doors.

*

The next morning I stood on the balcony in a light breeze. The slowly rising sun turned the mountains a deep purple and the water a shiny pink. I pulled on my skirt and sandals.

Andrew looked up sleepily from his pillow. "Where you going?"

"I have to go out to the desert. I'll be back in a couple of hours."

Andrew rubbed his eyes. "What? Now?" He glanced at his watch. "It's so early."

"I have to go before it gets too hot."

"Mia, wait. Please, don't go alone." Andrew sat up and grabbed my hand. "It's not safe."

"I've heard that before." I pulled away from him and filled my backpack with a box of crackers and several bottles of water.

We finally agreed he'd drive out with me but go for coffee with the driver while I walked alone.

I chose a taxi from the lineup on the street and arranged the price. The driver seemed a little confused. "But what do you want to see?"

"I just want to walk out into the desert."

The driver shrugged, and we got in the back of the cab. Andrew sat across from me, hidden behind his mirrored sunglasses. I couldn't tell if he was annoyed by my need for a desert field trip or just concerned. The taxi seats had lost their spring and I hung on to the handle above the door. Every bump sent a jolt up my spine.

The cab stopped a half hour later. "If you walk that way, you'll see nothing."

Andrew gave me a compass he kept on his backpack. "You promise you'll come back?"

I nodded, and then he and the driver drove off, leaving me on the road.

The morning quickly became scorching, but I was well hydrated. I looked at the compass, chose a direction and started walking in a straight line. Quickly I lost sight of the road. Just the horizon of light brown sand loomed ahead, with puffy clouds against the blue sky.

I sat down in the sand and sifted it through my fingers. Once I'd wanted to come and feel connected to God, but that seemed unimportant now. I wasn't sure who was seeking the connection. Yeshiva girl? Guitar-playing Mia? Andrew's lover? "Stop it," I said aloud. Stop stop stop. They were just layers, outfits I could take off. What was really at heart? I took a deep breath and tried to concentrate. What could I say for sure? I was flesh and blood, lungs and a heart. I was a girl, maybe a woman.

The sky stretched like a vast flat pancake. I felt very small, a speck on the desert, a microscopic bit in the atmosphere. The sun blazed down, the heat sucking away my jitteriness. I took another long drink from my water bottle. Then I lay in the sand and let the heat soak up into me, burning my skin through my clothes. I felt molten.

What else could I say? I was Jewish. I loved music and trees. I loved Andrew. I believed in social justice. I had responsibilities. I repeated these out loud. "Andrew, trees, music." I loved music. I was not whole without music. I got up from the sand and started to head back the way I'd come. I felt a little dizzy but also clear-headed. I repeated, "Andrew, trees, music," as I walked back to the road.

*

After the trip out to the desert, Andrew and I spent the mornings at the outdoor café of our hotel under a wooden sun umbrella. We sat at a low table, leaning back on colorful bolsters. I wore a bikini and sarong and a breeze blew my loose hair about my naked shoulders. A waiter brought us fresh coffee and rolls. I held Andrew's hand and he told me about surfing, about his mother. She was a breast-cancer survivor. He'd lived with her when she was sick, when he was in college. He told me about his job at a research lab, the apartment he'd chosen to be near both his mother and a surf beach, so he could watch over her and the waves.

When it got too hot we went up to our room and napped. In the late afternoons we swam, snorkeled and played guitar on the beach. Other travelers joined us, singing or pulling out little bongo drums or occasionally a guitar or harmonica.

At night, after beers or a joint on the beach, Andrew would read or sleep, and I would lie under a sheet so the air-conditioning wouldn't blow right on me. I tried to think about Aviva and Michelle in class, about the old women at the craft center. They felt so far away, like a novel I once read. I remembered the Hebrew songs I learned for choir. I whispered them aloud and felt them foreign on my tongue. My mind spun in loose circles, from the stolen trees to the house I helped rebuild to the bomb and back to the trees. Sometimes I seethed with energy and felt like pacing the room. Other times the information was like weights on my chest and I felt paralyzed.

On our last night in Dahab, Andrew and I sat on the balcony watching the sunset. Andrew ran his fingers through my hair. "So, you made any decisions about your school?"

I sighed. "I can't go back. I'm too distracted."

"By me?" Andrew tugged on my hair.

I pulled away from him. "Yes, by you, but also by Israel. There's so much I don't understand."

"Like?"

"I don't understand what an ancient bible story is supposed to mean to me now. There are some parts that are really great and other parts that are, well, outdated, I guess."

"Can't you just follow the parts you like and leave out the other stuff?"

"Maybe in some other community…but not at my school."

"All or nothing, huh?"

I nodded. We sat for a moment in silence.

Andrew squeezed my hand. "How did you ever become religious in the first place?"

"Oh." I sighed. "I wanted a normal family—"

Andrew burst out laughing.

"Why's that funny?"

"Do you know anyone whose family is normal? I mean really normal? Everyone's got something: their parents are divorced or dead or they're not talking to one of their siblings. Everyone's got something."

"Okay, well, I wanted a family that was together."

"Your dad?"

"Yeah, him. I thought if I was religious, I'd get married and have the kind of family that stuck together."

"Sounds like a good plan."

I shrugged. "Yeah, maybe for someone else." I froze a little as I said that. I knew I wasn't going to rejoin Aviva's family in Toronto, but saying it out loud made my stomach churn. I thought I might cry, but I felt too old and too tired.

The sun dipped over the horizon and I turned to face Andrew. "I'm going to do something else when we get back to Jerusalem."

Andrew raised one eyebrow at me.

"Rebuilding was great, but I want to do more."

"You wrote an amazing song. We taught it to some Palestinian children. That's something."

"I need to take more serious action."

"More rebuilding?"

"No."

Andrew frowned. "What are you saying?"

"Well…" I paused, trying to find the right words. "I've been thinking about that other group you told me about, the one that works with Palestinian families to help them keep their land."

Andrew let out a low whistle. "That could be really dangerous. I don't think—"

I put my hand up to stop him. "You don't have to come."

Andrew stared at me. I thought, We still barely know each other. Then he said, "You're serious, aren't you?"

I nodded. Andrew leaned back and folded his arms across his chest. He pressed his lips together. We sat looking at each other. Then he smiled and squeezed my hand. "You always do what you want, don't you?"

I wasn't sure what to say. He was right. I was the kind of person who jumped into things, who knew her mind. I nodded, and Andrew sighed and looked away from me, out at the waves.

The light was fading around us and the air was warm and balmy. I went into the room and got Andrew's guitar and started strumming "Crazy." I felt both nervous and excited.

Already my mind was humming with new lyrics about trees. Not decorative or planted, but trees that bore fruit, lost their leaves in the fall and made shade in the summer. I wanted to write music to evoke their holiness, or maybe the sound of wind in their branches. The words would make you think of God, of a creator of the most beautiful things. You could sing the song under a tree and look up and see the sky through the leaves and branches, and if other people sang with you, you could feel the same spiritual buzz as singing on Shabbos. I thought about sitting under the trees at Don's cottage with Andrew, playing Don a song Andrew and I wrote together. And maybe the song would be on banjo, a kind of low twangy sound. It could be called "Catch Your Breath."

"Do you know how to play mandolin?" I asked Andrew. He shook his head. "I'll have to teach you."

Andrew watched me, amused, as I did some old country picking.

"Do you know this song?" I played and sang "In the Highways," an old Maybelle Carter tune Don had taught me.

Andrew shook his head.

"You will soon. It goes like this."

243

GLOSSARY

Please note: Alternative spellings exist for many of these terms.

ba'al teshuva—literally "one who has returned," a formerly non-observant Jew who returns to the traditional ways of Judaism (also means reborn Jews)

beit midrash—"house of learning" or study hall

Birkot Hashahar—morning prayers

B'nos Sarah—"Daughters of Sarah," fictional name of the yeshiva or seminary Mia attends

bracha—blessing

b'shert—Yiddish for "destiny," refers to one's future spouse or soulmate

bubbie—the Yiddish word for "grandmother"

challah—braided bread eaten on the Sabbath (plural—*challot*)

chassid—a member of the ultra-Orthodox branch of Judaism

chevruta—a study partner for learning Jewish texts

Eretz Yisrael—the land of Israel

frum—Yiddish for "religious" or "observant"

gemilut hasadim—"giving loving kindness," refers to charitable acts

hamotzi—blessing recited before eating bread

haredi—ultra-Orthodox community

Hashem—God

havdalah—a ceremony using candles, wine and sweet spices that marks the end of the Sabbath

horah—a type of circle dance

Ir Hakodesh—"city of peace," refers to the spot in Jerusalem where the first temple was built

kadosh—holy

kibbutznik—a member of a *kibbutz*, a collective farming community

kippah—religious head covering traditionally worn only by men

Kotel—part of the massive remaining stone walls of the Second Temple; the *Kotel* is also called the Wailing or Western Wall and is the most sacred site in Judaism

kumzitz—from the Yiddish "*kum, zitz,*" meaning "come, sit"; refers to a sing-along

mameleh—Yiddish for "mother dear," a term of endearment

mellah—Arabic for a walled Jewish quarter of a city in Morocco

Mitzvot—"the commandments," the 613 principles of law and ethics outlined in the Torah

Moshe—Moses

Moshiach—the Messiah

Nakba—Arabic for "the catastrophe," when 650,000 to 750,000 Palestinians either fled or were expelled from their homes by Israeli forces in 1948

Rashi—Rabbi Shlomo Yitzchaki, foremost commentator on the Torah and Talmud

Ribbono shel Olam—"Master of the Universe," a way of referring to God

Shabbos/Shabbat—the day of rest and worship; for Jews this is Saturday

shidduch—a system of matchmaking where Jewish singles are introduced to each other for the purpose of marriage

shtetl—a Jewish town in pre-Holocaust Central and Eastern Europe

shuk—market

shul—Yiddish for "synagogue" or "temple"

Shulchan Aruch—literally "The Set Table," a book of Jewish law composed by Rabbi Yoséf Karo in the sixteenth century

tikkun olam— Hebrew for "repairing the world"

Torah—the law of God as revealed to Moses and recorded in the first five books of the Hebrew Scriptures; the first part of the Hebrew Bible

Tu B'shvat—"New Year of the Trees," a Jewish holiday celebrated by planting trees and eating dried fruits and nuts

yeshiva—a seminary or school for the study of Jewish texts

Yiddish—a language spoken by Eastern European Jews

zeydi—the Yiddish word for "grandfather"

AUTHOR'S NOTE

Like many young North American Jews, I grew up knowing very little about the Israeli occupation of Palestinian land. As a teenager I thought Israel was unpopulated until the Jews returned in the early twentieth century. When I visited Israel in 1995 as a university student, I had just read Leon Uris's *Exodus,* and I was thrilled to think of my visit to Israel as a homecoming. During my stay, I gradually became more aware of the political realities plaguing Israel, especially as terrorist attacks increased. However, it wasn't until I took a graduate course exploring the memory of Jews and Palestinians that I started to understand how Israel was created, and how the Jewish return to Israel uprooted native Palestinian populations. I was appalled to learn that more than 600,000 Palestinians had been forced into exile in 1948 and that many were still living as refugees in what had once been their own homeland.

I struggled with my new knowledge. I loved Israel and I wanted to believe Israel had a heroic and honorable history. How could I, a Jew, criticize the state after the centuries of oppression Jews had endured? Eventually, I decided to embrace the Jewish tradition of fighting for social justice and write this book. I believe Israel will be a stronger, more peaceful country when it follows international law and protects the human rights of all peoples within its borders. I pray for peace, but I believe it will only come when the occupation is ended.

Although I read many different books and articles during my research, I was particularly influenced by Carol Bardenstein's article "Trees, Forests, and the Shaping of Palestinian and Israeli Collective Memory" (in *Acts of Memory: Cultural Recall in the Present*, edited by Mieke Bal, Jonathan Crewe and Leo Spitzer), Sandy Tolan's *The Lemon Tree* and Jasmine Habib's *Israel, Diaspora and the Routes of National Belonging*.

ACKNOWLEDGMENTS

Many thanks to my talented Toronto writing group: Elizabeth MacLeod, Dianne Scott, Roswell Spafford, Ania Szado, Elsie Sze and Anne Warrick. In Kingston my friends Dorit Naaman and Sarah Tsiang also gave me valuable feedback.

I am indebted to Professor Lorenzo Buj for his course on memory, which got me interested in the Israel/Palestine conflict.

Thanks to my editor, Sarah Harvey, for helping bring this book into focus.

I am extremely grateful to the Ontario Arts Council and the Canada Council for the Arts for their support.

Special thanks to Tawfiq Zayyad's widow, Naela Zayyad, for granting me permission to quote from her husband's poem "On the Trunk of an Olive Tree," originally published in *al-A'mal al-Kamila* (Complete Works) by Dar al-Aswar Publishers.

Lastly, many thanks to my husband, Rob, for enduring many conversations like this:

Me: So I'm thinking about Mia.

Him: Who?

Me: You know, the main character of my book.

Him: Her again? Still?

Rob, your patience and support is much appreciated.

LEANNE LIEBERMAN is the author of *Gravity*, a Sydney Taylor Notable Book for Teens. Leanne is from Vancouver but now lives in Kingston, Ontario, with her husband and two sons. She lived in Israel in 1995 and again in 1999.